The *BOAT THIEF*

By M.D. Lee

~ *To my M's* ~

Special Thanks to:
Andy, Bob, Becky, Mary, Tim, Noel

Prologue

Most people don't know the exact time they're going to die. I do. Two hours and ten minutes from now. 3:47 p.m. Lucky me.

There's nothing I can do about it. There's nothing anyone can do about it. There's not another person around for ten or twenty miles who can help.

But here I am, waiting to die. At thirteen.

How did things get so messed up, that I'm stuck in this situation? Was it all because of a dumb kiss? Probably not.

The sea is now only about six or seven feet from my face, but slowly, very slowly, the tide will creep back and, like some evil serpent, swallow me whole.

My parents and friends will never know what happened. I doubt anyone will ever find anything left after the sea gets through with me.

So alone. I've never felt so alone in my life.

I smile weakly as I think about how it was only last week I was sitting in social studies, daydreaming of being anywhere but there. Well, this is certainly anywhere but there. As much as I hate social studies, I'd rather be there than here. Instead, I'm stuck face down in the damp sand, knowing that soon I'll be underwater.

« CHAPTER 1 »

Hiding out

It's the summer of 1978, here in Maine, and unknown to me, things are about to happen that will change my life forever.

I'm a scrawny thirteen year old, smaller than most kids my age. My pants look like I need to grow into them, and my button-down shirt always seems too loose. Other than the scrawny part, I really couldn't care less how my clothes fit. My name is Fisher Shoemaker.

I wait all school year for that last day because summertime is *my* time. I can finally get out of the stuffy classroom and be free. These final days, nine days to be exact, but who's counting, with the weather getting nice, time moves *so* painfully slow; the grass has turned green, and for about a month now the leaves have been out. The green leaves taunt me. In the first part of spring, I seem to be the only one to notice the air has the smell of fresh-cut grass. It's morally wrong to keep a kid locked up in a classroom on a beautiful spring day. It just isn't right.

"Fisher!" My teacher's voice pierces my brain and I drag my gaze from the window. She looks hard at me from the front of the classroom. She is not smiling. She's wearing thick horn-rimmed glasses, and her hair's wound up in a bun that seems painfully tight. The dress she's wearing is boring blue: like she's working for the prison system. I'm her inmate.

"What is the answer to number seven, Fisher?" I look blankly at her, then at the other kids. Are any of them are going to help me out? Or are they just going to let me hang? They let me hang. I have no idea what we're even talking about, and I'm only vaguely aware that I'm in social studies.

She stares hard at me with cold eyes while tapping her pencil on the desk. "Do you even know what we're discussing today?" she growls. I say nothing. The other kids don't laugh, or blurt out the right answers; they're just glad she's picking on me and not them.

"Fisher Shoemaker, you really need to pay more attention. I know you don't think so, but social studies is important. It'll help you evolve into an adult who is more aware of the world around him."

An adult? I'm really not worried about becoming an adult. At least, the thought has never occurred to me before. Why should I worry about it now? There're better things to think about. All I'm really interested in is getting out of this dang classroom so I can work on my hideout. It's down by the beachhead near Goosewing Rock. My bike is right outside, in the schoolyard, waiting to take me away from all this.

But I can't stop thinking about what the teacher said. This is the first time the idea of becoming an adult has ever been brought to my attention . . . and I don't like it. What does it mean? Am I going to have to go out and get a job soon to support myself? Is my dad going to tell me I need to move out of the house? Will I still like building forts and hideouts, or is that just not allowed? Damn that teacher for even mentioning it.

"Fisher, I want you to read chapter three again tonight and answer the four questions at the back of the chapter to turn in before class tomorrow. Do you understand?"

I nod my head yes, knowing full well I am never going to look at chapter three. I'm just going to have to suffer the consequences tomorrow. Somehow I think she knows this as she stands up, looking madder than I have ever seen her. With her yardstick pointing straight at me, she barks, "Fisher! . . ."

Suddenly, from the back of the classroom, "PTHHHHHH!" It's loud, like someone just cut one! The whole classroom erupts in laughter.

"Class! Class! Stop this laughing at once!" the teacher shouts. But it's too late; she's lost control. Seconds later the bell rings and, in an instant, social studies and chapter three are just fading memories. Thank God.

As the room empties, Tommy Goodwell yells over to me, with a sly grin on his face, "You owe me one, Shoemaker." I salute back to him. Tommy Goodwell makes the best fart noises—the whole school knows it. He just saved my butt.

My trusty Schwinn five-speed, with a deep blue paint job and locked to the bike stand closest to the trees, is right where I left it. My bike takes me everywhere—over to friends' houses, to the corner store in town, to the docks where I watch the lobstermen, to the ball-field, and just about everywhere else my mom doesn't feel like driving me. It's more than just a bike to me. It's my freedom.

As I'm turning the dial on the combo lock, Jimmy Hinns calls from where his bike's parked. "My brother just got the new Led Zeppelin album. Want to come over and listen to it on my dad's stereo? He's not home now, but he'd go crazy if he heard Led Zeppelin coming out of his new speakers." He smirks.

Jimmy's one of those kids whose parents let him do anything. Like band members on the back of album covers, his hair's long. He even gets to wear bell-bottom jeans to school. Not me. I have a short haircut and "school clothes."

"David Small's coming over, too. He's gonna bring those two girls from science class," Jimmy says.

Hanging out with two girls doesn't sound like all that much fun to me. Most girls really only want to talk about clothes and other boys. For the most part, they're just plain annoying.

"No thanks. I'm gonna go work on my hideout instead."

Hopping on his bike, Jimmy just rolls his eyes and shakes his head.

Besides, as far as I can tell, I'm not what most girls my age find interesting. I'm only about the size of a large grade-school kid, and my dad still cuts my hair. The result looks like he used a bowl with dull hedging shears. He's no barber, but he's able to save a couple of bucks doing it himself. Honestly, in the end, I really don't care what I look like.

∞ ∞ ∞

Trent Harbor, Maine. It's where I live. It's like almost every other small town on the East Coast. Everything in it is about lobsters and summer tourists; that's how almost everyone here makes their money. They catch lobsters, then feed them to the summer people. There're probably a dozen lobster boats moored in the harbor, and there are almost as many seafood restaurants. And if the lobsters don't catch the tourists, there are plenty of gift shops that'll try to lure them in.

What the tourists don't like, when the wind direction is just right, is the pungent odor of bait cooking in the summer sun down at the town dock. It wafts up Main Street, giving the town a very powerful fishy smell. Honestly, some days I don't like it either, and it's all I can do to keep from tossing my lunch. But it's not always like that. Sometimes the wind blows the other way, and there's nothing but fresh sea mustiness. I sort of like it.

At the end of Main, beyond all the shops and restaurants, is a dirt road that leads to the town dock. The lobstermen use the dock to offload their catch. Half of it is taken up by walls of lobster traps stacked high. Nearby is a pile of colored buoys. Below the tall wooden pilings, floating docks move up and down with the tide and are lined with small dinghies people use to row out to their boats on moorings.

To get to my hideout I have to pass by the sailing club. It's just a little past the town dock where most of us kids hang out in the summer. Only after passing the tests can we take a sailboat out on our own. I'm a pretty good sailor, if I do say so myself. I've advanced all the way through, passing my solo test, and I'm one of the few younger kids allowed to take a boat alone. Next summer I'll probably take my instructor test. But it actually seems like too much bother, when I can just as easily take a boat out whenever I please and not worry about teaching someone else.

The sailing club is actually just an old garage at the water's edge covered with cedar shingles. It's perfect for holding sails, life jackets, and a few other odds and ends that go with a sailboat. Inside, the hard cement floor's always damp from wet life jackets drying out, and has a permanent smell like something rotting in soft black dirt. In the back is an office. It's actually just an old desk with an overhead light where the older boys pretend to be doing some sort of work, but are really just looking at girls in swimsuit magazines. Outside, a neat little patch of grass is used by the instructors; in the morning for lessons and for folding sails in the afternoon.

Because all I can think about is finishing up the roof, I'm anxious to get to my hideout. First, though, I stop at the boat ramp to see who's going sailing; but only for a second. At the gate I get off my bike to have a look around. There're only two younger kids, who I really don't know because they're two grades behind me, setting up a boat,. There's no reason for me to hang out here any longer. I turn back to my bike to go.

"Fisher!" A girl's calling me from the far row of boats. I hadn't noticed her before, and now that I see her I secretly wish I hadn't stopped at the club. I lower my head pretending not to hear.

It's Sara Banks. She's about my age, yet I really don't know her because throughout the years she's always been in a different class. Growing up, I thought she was kind of weird because she had scraggly hair, and she wore her older sister's clothes that look a size too big and a few years out of style. As far as I can tell she doesn't have too many friends, either, because she always seems to be by herself. Today though, when I look at her, there's something different about her. For some reason she doesn't look as weird as she had before. Maybe it's because her brown hair's in a neat ponytail, or her clothes actually seem to fit her. I really don't know what it is.

7

"Are you going sailing today?" she calls out from the last sailboat that's sitting up on the ramp.

"No. I'm going down to my . . ." then I stop myself and squirm a little. I don't want to tell her about my hideout because she'll think I'm too old to be playing in forts and hideouts. Besides, a hideout's a secret and I don't want anyone, especially a girl, knowing where it is. "No, I'm going home to watch some TV." It sounds dumb coming out of my mouth, especially since my house is in the other direction.

She looks at me strangely, probably knowing I just made that up, and then says, "I need someone who's passed their solo test to go sailing with me. I saw your name on the list; do you want to go?" She gives me a little smile then she walks over closer to where I'm standing.

"No, I really can't. I have things to do," I say, hoping she'll take the hint and leave it alone.

"But it's such a great afternoon for sailing. Just take me out for a little bit. I really need the practice," she says.

She's right. It's a nice afternoon, but today's the day I'm going to put the roof on the hideout. I've been collecting wood from all over town and I finally have enough to start the job. I've been planning on this for a long time, and I'm not going to let some dumb girl stop me.

"Not today, maybe some other time," I say, shifting back

8

and forth anxiously on my feet.

Sara gives me a little poke on my shoulder. "Oh, come on. Just go sailing with me for a little while. There's nobody else here who can take a boat out on their own."

I don't really hear the last part she said because I'm thinking about how she just touched me on the shoulder. In my mind I know I should be grossed out that a girl like Sara Banks has touched me on the shoulder, but I'm not. I feel strange.

Why can't she just leave it alone? I really don't want to sail today, and I'm certainly not going to let her keep me from putting the roof on my hideout. And on top of all that, I'm suddenly feeling strange about being near her. I need to leave . . . now!

I wave her off and swing my leg over the bike, "Tomorrow we can go for a sail. I promise."

I pump the pedals hard like a bike racer on the starting line. Damn . . .why did I say that? What if I don't get the roof done this afternoon and need to work on it tomorrow?

I'm still riding my bike as fast as I can, sweat beginning to build on my back, when I get to the edge of town. I turn left down a road no one uses much anymore, where weeds push up through cracks in the pavement. After a mile or so, I come to the dead end and lift my bike over the rusty lock and chain meant to keep out intruders like me. Two tracks, overgrown with grass and littered with twigs, lead down to the water's edge. There, a narrow path angles off toward a grouping of large rocks and boulders, just above the high tide mark, that looks as if a giant has stacked them. It's between these rocks where I'm building my hideout. No one knows of this place.

All good hideouts need protection. I came up with several systems that should keep the bad guys out. Several yards away from the entrance door I have two smaller pine trees bent down and held in place with a light line. If I look out the peephole and see someone I don't like, I simply cut the line. The pines will explode, whipping across the path, sending the bad guy into the next county. If they get past that, I'll use the backup booby trap. Above the door I have a crate filled with heavy rocks. All I need to do is tug on the rope that hangs by the door, and the rocks will flatten anyone standing there. Don't mess with me.

But that's not all. If I'm being attacked from the ocean side, I have several slingshots by the window opening. Next to the window I have a pail of small round rocks ready to fire. I've been practicing. I should be able to nail anyone coming at me from that direction.

The hideout looks out over the rocky harbor where many boats are kept on their moorings. Past the mooring field is a scattering of smaller islands with nothing more than a few tall pines and a couple of large boulders. Beyond that's open ocean. I can see white splashes of water shooting into the air from the lumbering swells hitting hard rock. Also, there're many sea birds and gulls all screeching as they search the shore for food. This is the perfect place for a hideout; at least that's what I think.

My lumber's stashed away, stacked in a neat pile just off to the side in some tall grass, so should anyone walk along the shore's edge they'd never see it. I pull a few pieces out and begin measuring. I've got a lot of work ahead of me and only a few hours before I need to be home for dinner.

The daylight begins to fade and soon the damp sea air creeps in, almost unnoticed. I need to head home for dinner. Looking over the day's work, I realize I've only nailed down two roof planks. Am I being lazy? Maybe. I wish I'd gotten farther, but I'm pleased with how it's turning out. I must've been doing too much daydreaming and not enough work. Well, it's my hideout, I'm in charge, and I can work as slow as I please and no one can tell me otherwise. I just sigh. I'm going to need to keep working on it tomorrow, but I promised Sara I would take her sailing. Time to go.

It's probably too dark for me to be riding my bike, but the town's pretty quiet and there are no cars on the road. I think I'm safe riding in the fading light. In the darkness, lights inside homes are coming on and I can see families are getting ready for dinner. I better hurry.

Just before turning right on Main Street is the steepest hill in town. It's almost impossible to ride up on a bike, but I've done it

11

before. I already have my bike in the lowest gear, and need to pedal standing up if I'm going to make it to the top. There's a sense of pride being one of the few kids who can get there without having to give up and walk.

Near the top of the hill, I realize there's someone walking in the street. Because I'm concentrating hard on keeping the bike moving, I hadn't noticed him before. Suddenly he turns around as I'm about to pass him.

"Shoemaker!" With a sick feeling, I recognize the voice about the same time his hand lashes out, grabbing my hand brake and bringing me to a violent stop.

"Ooof!" I grunt as I launch off the seat abruptly, straddling the crossbar in an extremely painful way.

Standing before me wearing a black T-shirt and jeans, with a half cigarette hanging out of his mouth, is Owen Scaggs.

His greasy, long hair hides all the oozing pimples on his face. His eyes are dark, like a snake, revealing little about himself. He's only a little bigger than me, and surely he's stronger, but I don't want to find out. Nobody at school really knows much about him, and there's a rumor that he once was sent to juvenile prison. Nobody really knows for sure.

He flicks an ash and enjoys the look of terror on my face. For some reason, I can't speak and it feels like hours before Owen finally says something. "How much money do you have on you?"

12

"None," I say, wishing I had at least some change, or something, to give him, just so I can escape without getting hurt.

"I don't believe you," he says, and with one quick shove I'm on the ground with my bike on top of me. "I really don't understand," he continues. "This happens all the time. I ask stupid kids like you nicely for some money, and you think I'm so dumb that if you tell me you have no money, I'll just go away. That's not how this game works." He stands on my hand, pinning it in place.

With pain shooting through my hand, my face scrunches up tight as he presses even harder with his foot.

"Let me ask you again; how much money do you have on you?"

I'm glad none of my friends can see me, because I think there may be tears running down my face. At this point I don't even care.

"I told you the truth. I don't have any money on me," I say through clenched teeth. Oh, the pain; Owen Scaggs steps even harder on my hand.

He doesn't say anything for a second, grinning hard, and thinking about what I said. "I'm really sorry; I thought you were lying to me." He lifts my bike off me. "Here, let me help you up." He even puts out his hand to help me off the ground, but the smirk never leaves his face, which makes me feel like this isn't over.

Again we stand facing each other, not saying anything. He

cautiously takes a look around to see if any of the neighbors are watching.

"This is a really nice bike," he says, finally. "What is it—a Schwinn? I think I'll take this instead of the money. I don't really like the blue; maybe I'll spray paint it black."

Suddenly, all in one move, Owen Scaggs swiftly swings his leg over the bike, then sidekicks me to the stomach. For a second time I hit the ground.

"If you're smart, you won't tell anyone I took your bike. You know I'll get you if you do. And I might not be as nice next time."

Before I can even stand up he's already flying down the hill on the bike that I bought with my own money. What am I going to do now? How am I going to get around? What am I going to tell my parents? If I'd left my hideout just a little sooner, I might've missed Owen Scaggs altogether. I throw a rock at the stop sign . . . but miss. "Damn it!"

« CHAPTER 2 »
Splash

Because I had to walk the rest of the way home last night, it gave me some time to think. I decided I can't tell my dad my bike was stolen because he'll be mad that I didn't stand up for myself. But it was Owen Scaggs. No one messes with Owen Scaggs. Sooner or later, though, Dad's going to ask about the bike. I have no idea what to tell him. Luckily, I made it to the dinner table on time last night, so there was no reason for him to notice. I'm just going to have to forget about the bike until I save enough for a new one.

Today isn't starting out great. Without a bike, I'm forced to either ride the bus to school or walk. I decide to walk. If my dad sees me waiting for the bus, I figure he'll ask me why I'm not riding my bike to school. The problem is, it's taken me longer to walk than I thought, so now I'm late, and earn myself an after-school detention. It's not a big deal. The detention's only a half hour, but yesterday I promised Sara Banks I would take her sailing today. If I'm a half hour late, maybe she'll give up waiting and go home. If she doesn't, at least maybe by that time no one will be around to see me sailing with Sara Banks. I'm hoping she'll just leave because then I can finish up the roof on my hideout.

Once again I find myself in front of the sailing club, and there's Sara waiting patiently by the boat. She's carefully rigged the sails, and two life jackets sit in the cockpit. I let out a sigh and look around to if see any of my friends are around to see me. The only person who notices me is Sara.

"Fisher, what took you so long? I got the boat set up while I was waiting." She looks at me as if expecting me to say something, but I'm not in the mood.

"Well?"

"Well, what?" I say.

"How do you think I did setting up the boat? I've never set one up by myself, but I've helped others a lot," she says with a proud smile.

I look over her work. The jib's hanked on to the forestay and stacked in a neat pile on the bow, and the jib sheets are attached with clean bowline knots. She's also done the same thing to the mainsail, flaking it neatly to the boom. She's coiled all the extra lines in the cockpit in neat circles, paying particular attention to keeping them from knotting up on each other. Not bad for a girl, I think.

"You did alright, I guess." I point to one of the lines, "You probably should've put a stopper knot in the end of that one so it doesn't get away." That doesn't discourage her as she quickly puts a figure-eight knot onto the end.

"Can we go now?" she asks.

16

"Yes," I say, and I'm actually beginning to feel better about the day. After all, it's better than being in school and it's a sunny clear day with a building sea breeze. Sailing a boat is always better than sitting at a desk.

Both of us grab hold on either side of the sailboat and, in one move, slide it off the wooden ramp and into the water. Sara hops in first, and I give the boat a little shove from the dock, hopping in, too. I turn to her and say, "You take the tiller and steer us away from the dock."

She looks at me with surprise and then beams. "I've never done that before," she says. "But I know I can do it because I've practiced it a lot out in the harbor." She grabs hold of the tiller and mainsheet and concentrates on the job at hand. That leaves me tending to the jib, making sure the sail is trimmed properly.

The wind's light, but it's still enough to push the little boat through the water. When the breeze fills the sails, the boat heels over, tipping to one side. To help balance out the boat, we both sit on the high side. As she steers around the moored boats, frowning slightly as she concentrates, I can see she actually knows what she's doing. Once out in the open harbor, clear from anything that can get in our way, Sara eases up a bit and begins to looking around.

"This is such a great place to sail. Look at all these islands and things we could explore." She's right; there're lots of islands we can explore. But growing up here I guess I never paid too much attention to the idea of exploring the islands, or anywhere else, for that matter. People have built homes on some islands, but there're many other smaller ones that are deserted. "Maybe we can have a picnic on one of them someday," she says, smiling.

I'm not so sure about that idea.

When we're out farther, past the last entrance buoy, the wind's a little stronger. The boat begins to heel more; yet, without me having to tell her, Sara eases the traveler car down so the boat will flatten out a little nicer. Not bad, I think. She's paying attention to what she's supposed to be doing.

Now that we're out in the bay, I'm able to sight along the shore to where my hideout's situated. Just as I'd hoped, unless someone knows right where it is, no one's going to be able to spot it.

"What are you looking at?" Sara asks, breaking my daze.

"Nothing," I say.

"You know, you don't talk very much. I'm going to start thinking you're one of those weird boys who always seem to get shoved into school lockers. You're not, are you?"

I look at her, not saying anything. Maybe she's right, but who is she to judge when she doesn't even know me? I take a quick second glance just to make sure I still can't see my hideout out here on the water.

"There! I saw you. You are clearly looking at something. Don't tell me you weren't, Fisher Shoemaker."

I suppose I can trust her . . . maybe. But she's a girl, after all, and will surely blab to all her friends about my hideout. But I'm sick of all her questions, so I give up. Raising my hand, I point to a big rock far off in the distance near shore. "There, see that large rock, just to the left of the tree that looks like it's falling over?"

Sara glances quickly in that direction while trying not to take her eyes off the direction we're sailing. "I think so," she says.

"That's my hideout, tucked in behind that rock."

She takes another quick look, and then faces me.

"You have a hideout? I don't see anything," she says. I roll my eyes. Girls!

"You're not supposed to see anything, that's why it's called a hideout."

"Why don't you show it to me after we're done sailing," she says with a smile.

Crap. I hadn't thought she'd want to see it. I can't let her near it; she might show it to someone. I look at the jib and make some adjustments to the sail, pretending I don't hear her.

"What? Are you afraid I might show someone your little fort?" she says, grinning again. How does she know that? Are all girls like her?

"No, I just can't show it to you, that's all," I say, knowing she isn't going to let it drop. The last thing I want is to have Sara Banks hanging out at my hideout. Before I know what happened she'll

19

probably have all her friends there, too.

Suddenly I reach out for the tiller and pull it hard to starboard. "Watch out for that lobster pot," I scream. There's no lobster pot, but I need to get her mind off my hideout.

I must've pulled the tiller harder than I thought. The boat rounds up sharply, heeling it almost on its side as water comes rushing in over the splashboards. In the same instant, I see Sara's feet go straight up in the air as she plunges backwards, splashing into the water. The boat quickly leaves her behind in its wake. Damn! Now I've done it. I've lost Sara overboard.

Part of the test to take a sailboat out by myself was to practice and pass the man-overboard drills. I'd passed the test perfectly, retrieving the life ring the instructor tossed overboard, which was supposed to be a person. Picking Sara out of the water shouldn't be any harder.

Without Sara controlling the mainsail it's flogging violently in the wind, making a loud racket. Quickly grabbing hold of the mainsheet, I pull it tight, bringing the sail back under control. With the tiller in hand, I steer the sailboat back around, as I've practiced a hundred times before, so I can pluck Sara out of the water.

The little boat swings around in a big circle just a little downwind of her, and I can easily see the life jacket holding her head above water. Sara isn't in any real danger, but she's not smiling either. With the boat pointing directly into the wind, it glides to almost a stop right alongside her. I'm able to get a hand on the life jacket to pull her aboard. Plop! She hits the floorboards, leaving a big puddle of saltwater around her. She's in a wet heap, and her sopping clothes cling to her skin. Sara lies there for a moment as she catches her breath. The water's cold this time of year, and she begins to shiver a little.

Her wet hair's matted to her face when she gets up off the floorboards. "You big turd!" she screams with fire coming out of her eyes, and slugs me in the shoulder. "Why'd you do that? There was no lobster pot in the way, and you know it." Her eyes have turned from raging mad to hurt, like someone just told her that her dog died. I can't look at her. My stomach feels uneasy.

Finally, I say, "I wanted you to stop asking me about my hideout."

"Why?" Her face is beginning to quiver, and then tears begin to roll down her wet face. "I thought you liked me, and maybe someday you'd show me your hideout." She wipes back some of the tears with the back of her soggy shirt sleeve. It doesn't help much.

"I don't know," I say, looking down at my feet. It's a horrible moment. Why didn't she just let it drop? She could clearly see that I didn't want to show it to her. But her tears are getting to me. I need to fix this. I think about it a second longer, then look at her and say, "I'll take you there when I'm done with the roof."

She squints her eyes hard at me and says, "Okay, you better,

21

or you'll be in big trouble, Fisher Shoemaker." She still looks hurt.

"We better head back. You're going to freeze if we don't get back soon." With that, I turn the sailboat around, tighten up the sails, and sail back to the club, which is now about a mile away.

« CHAPTER 3 »

Vanishing Vacation

Without a bike it now takes me a lot longer to get home from the sailing club. I still can't believe that scumbag, Owen Scaggs, helped himself to my bike. But what was I going to do? Only a dumb kid would try to stop him. And worst of all, at some point I'm going to have to face my dad. He's going to ask me where my bike is. Maybe I'm better off without it. But I know that's not true.

The long walk's given me time to wonder about Sara. I feel really bad that she ended up in the water. Now she's mad at me. By promising to show her my hideout maybe it'll make her less mad. Why'd she want me to take her sailing, anyway? There're plenty of other boys at the sailing club.

I arrive home just in time. I can see in the dining room Mom has the table already set, and parked in the driveway is my dad's big four-door Chevy Caprice Classic. Dad is home.

He loves that big car! It's push-button luxury. Secretly I wish he had something cooler; something like the black Mustang Steve McQueen drove in the movie "Bullet." Now *there's* a cool car. But honestly, I really can't see my dad driving a black Mustang to work. He's an accountant for one of the law firms in town, so a car that oozes luxury and practicality is more his speed. In any case, no matter how many times I picture it in my head, I just cannot see him pulling into his work space in a shiny black Mustang with an engine sounding like it'll tear apart anyone who gets in the way. It's just not him. Besides, his Sears business suits just wouldn't go with a cool car. My dad's a hard-working, practical guy and he drives a car that a hard-working, practical guy should drive.

He's also one of those guys who has all kinds of practical sayings. "A penny saved is a penny earned." And the one I don't understand: "Brains not brawn." What the heck does that mean? Why can't he just say what he means?

But, for the most part, he's a pretty good guy. Most of my friends like him. The trouble is, he thinks I'm lazy. If I'm sitting around, maybe watching television, he feels obligated to give me something to do. Unfortunately, it's usually chores around the house. It can be anything from cutting the lawn, to painting the old shed in the back. Sometimes I wonder if that's because when he was young there was no television where a kid could just sit and enjoy watching a favorite program. I think maybe they had radio to listen to. Spending the summer at my hideout is going to be the answer for avoiding my dad and all his crazy chores.

The hideout's going to be such a useful place; no one will be able to find me and put me to work. It's my summer vacation, and I want to spend it my way. Besides, what's the point of having summer vacation if I have to do a bunch of work, like weeding the garden? If that's the case, I think I'd almost rather be in the classroom staring out the window.

On the stove a pot boils, and through a cloud of steam my mom calls out to me, "Get washed up for dinner, and call your sister out of her room."

My mom still looks like June Cleaver, and refuses to wear any of the cool seventies clothes my other friends' moms are wearing. No lime-green pant suits for her. For as long as I can remember, she's always worn a house dress, usually accompanied by her favorite pale-pink apron that's stitched in flowers. Her hair, short and sensible, never in her face, always has that straight-from-the-parlor look. In fact, it's styled in such a way that I'm not even sure her hair moves.

We all sit down at the dinner table, with me and my sister sitting across from each other. My mom sits at one end, and at the head of the table, like the captain of his ship, sits Dad. He's still in his tie, but at this point in the day the jacket came off hours ago, and his long sleeves are rolled up. His eyeglasses are the good old black plastic, not the stylish wire-rimmed glasses everyone else is starting to wear. He says he doesn't want to look like that hippie, John Lennon.

"I saw you walking down Newbury Street this afternoon," my dad says before digging into his dinner. "How come you weren't riding your bike?"

I slouch in my chair, sigh, and give the spoon a little spin while I think up an answer other than "it was stolen."

"I let Tommy Olin borrow it. He was late for baseball practice, and needed to get across town fast."

"How come you aren't playing baseball this summer, Fisher?" Dad asks, instantly forgetting about the bike.

Here we go. He's going to start up with all the questions he already knows the answers to. Not really realizing I'm doing it, I thump my fingers on the table.

"I don't know. I just don't feel like it."

"What kind of a boy doesn't want to play baseball in the summer?" he asks with a scowl on his face, the kind where it looks like his eyebrow is going to curl up and fall off.

My dad looks up from the piece of meatloaf that he's just cut, and continues, "Fisher, you're thirteen this summer, and I think it's a good idea for you to have a summer job. It's time for you to learn about making money. If you aren't going to play baseball, then you should at least have a job."

That gets my attention! "Why do I have to get a job?" I protest. "None of my friends have jobs." The first thing that goes through my mind is my hideout. My big summer plan just got flushed down the toilet. A summer job will just not fit at all into my plan.

"I arranged for you to talk to Mrs. Fennel tomorrow, after school," my dad says. "You know Jack Fennel, her son. I think he's in your grade," he says, taking a bite of meatloaf.

So if he already made arrangements tomorrow for me to talk with Mrs. Fennel, he knew I wasn't going to play baseball this summer. I put my knife and fork down. This isn't fair!

The Fennel family owns a local restaurant called the Sea Side. It's not all that fancy, but it's where all the summer tourists go for a Maine lobster dinner and fried clams. Everyone sits on bench seats with newspaper spread across the tables. The newspaper makes it easy for the waitresses to clean up, because eating lobster is such a mess. It's a really busy place in the summer.

I push the peas around my plate, making little rows of green.

"But Dad," I protest. "I don't have time for a job this summer."

He chuckles and takes a bite of mashed potatoes, then says, "How can you possibly not have enough time? That's all you've got in the summer, is time. Mrs. Fennel is doing me a favor by taking you on in the restaurant. Tomorrow after school you need to stop by there and talk with her."

I start to object, but he puts his hand up and says, "Tomorrow she'll tell you when you start, and what you'll be doing. Remember, tomorrow after school." To emphasize his point, he waves an empty fork at me.

In some hot kitchen doing dishes on a sunny summer day is the last place I want to be! I hate doing dishes. I'm going to have to try to figure a way out of this one, but I know it's probably pointless because when my dad makes up his mind, that is that. Tomorrow I'll have to talk to Mrs. Fennel, like it or not.

« CHAPTER 4 »

First Time

My summer's started, but it's not the way I planned it. Last week I stopped in to talk with Mrs. Fennel at the Sea Side, just as my dad instructed me to do. She seems nice enough, and is happy I'm going to be starting as a dishwasher. I wish I was as happy. School ended a week ago, so tomorrow is going to be my first day on the job. Lucky me.

I'll be starting my job as a dishwasher and, if everything goes well, they'll train me to be a busboy. I have to admit, being a busboy actually sounds promising because Mrs. Fennel says if I hustle, and do a bang-up job, the waitresses have to split some of their tips with me. Tips? I hadn't thought about that when my dad told me about the job. But a little extra pocket change means I might be able to buy a new bike sooner than I thought.

Damn that Owen Scaggs.

Before school ended, I was able to finish the roof on my hideout. I'm excited that I got it done, but I doubt that I'll be able to spend any time there now that I'm employed.

Today, however, as promised after I accidentally lost her overboard, I'm going to take Sara Banks to see my hideout. I'm

29

meeting her by the sailing club. I still am not sure that's a good idea, but she was crying and wet at the time; what was I supposed to do? But I'm proud of the way it turned out, so I'm kinda looking forward to showing it to someone, even if it's only Sara Banks.

Stretched across two of the large boulders, wooden planks make up the hideout's roof. Even on the rainiest days it's as dry as any house roof. When I was done building, I'd found an old picnic table, which, after a fresh coat of paint, fit perfectly inside. Also, through what I call The Window (but is really just a big opening), there's somewhat of a good view of the harbor. But the real treasure is the old, small sofa. I scavenged it from the dump. A borrowed wheelbarrow made it easy to get it to my hideout, and, with a good brushing, and airing out, it is perfect. Part of me secretly can't wait to see what Sara thinks about the hideout.

Sara's waiting for me right outside the fence by the club, just as we'd decided. She gives me a little wave and a smile. "Hi Fisher," she says.

Today she looks different from how she usually looks in school. Not too bad, actually. Her hair, which is sandy brown, is not in a ponytail or anything; it's just sort of flowing. At school I've never seen her wear her hair like this. And she even has on a new pair of jeans instead of hand-me-downs. Honestly, she doesn't look like the Sara Banks everyone knows at school. I kind of like it.

As we're walking, we don't say much. She comments on

what a nice day it is, and I agree with her. Then Sara tells me about a friend of hers at school who did something funny at lunch with her sandwich, but I'm not really paying attention. For some reason, I'm feeling a little self-conscious about the way I look, yet Sara doesn't seem to mind. I can't understand why I really care how Sara thinks I look, but for some reason I do. It's strange. I promise myself next time I'm going to look a little better; maybe even comb my hair. All my friends are starting to comb their hair, maybe I should, too.

The hideout's only about a fifteen-minute walk from the sailing club, yet it's tucked away down a path nobody ever uses. Arriving at the old rusty chain across the overgrown road, I lift it up so she can pass under it. Attempting to be funny, I act like an English gentleman holding a door open for a lady. It's actually pretty lame, but she smiles and says, "Thank you, kind sir." As she passes under, she gives my shoulder a little squeeze.

Down toward the water's edge we're almost at the entrance to my hideout. I hold my hand up for her to stop. "Take a look around, do you see it?" I ask.

"See what?" she says.

"My hideout. You can't see it from here, can you?"

She looks harder, then I point right at the opening. "I still don't see anything," Sara says.

"That's perfect. I don't want anyone to know it's here. Come on," I say, as I almost grab her hand; but stop when I realize what

31

I'd almost done. I almost held her hand!

The entrance to the hideout is an actual door I found alongside the road, but I cleverly nailed pieces of pine branches to the front of it so it looks more like a tree than a door.

"Whoa! That's so cool." Sara says. "No one will ever know it's a door to a hideout." She looks it over until she's certain that I hadn't missed a spot with a pine branch. "I like how you have all the branches laid in there just like a real tree."

I swing the door open. She steps in and inspects the table and bench I've cleaned up and painted; she bangs on it twice with her fist. When she sees the old sofa in the corner by the window she laughs. "I can't believe you have an old couch in here. How did you get that thing in here?"

She looks around with satisfaction, putting her hands on her hips, and says, "I know what this place needs." Sara goes over to the far corner, where I had put all my empty Pepsi bottles, grabs one, and places it in the center of the table. Next, she goes back outside for almost a minute before returning with something in her hands that she keeps me from seeing.

As she places a bunch of daisies in the Pepsi-bottle vase, I realize that she hasn't been in my hideout for more than a minute, and already she has flowers in it. Girls! I feel like I should be more upset than I really am. The daisies aren't all that bad, and they do make the place look a little nicer, but I sure the hell am not going to let her know that.

"Get those things out of here," I say, but not very forcefully.

"Nope," she says in a very matter-of-fact tone.

"This is such a great place," she says. "What are you planning on doing with it?"

"I don't know. It's just a place to hang out. Now that I'm going to be working at the Sea Side I won't be able to get here as much as I thought I would."

Her eyes go wide, "You're working at the Sea Side? What are you doing there?"

Scratching at the ground with a stick, I say, "I'm just a dishwasher. But after a while I'll be training to be a busboy. That'll be cool because then I'll get some of the waitresses' tips."

"Maybe I should work there as a waitress," Sara says, smiling.

Why would anyone want to work on summer vacation if they didn't have to? It doesn't make sense "I think you have to be older to be a waitress. And I think they hired me as a favor to my dad."

I sit down on the sofa and put my feet up on the bench. I'm starting to really like my hideout.

Sara and I don't speak for a minute or two. It just seems nice hanging out in a place all my own with nothing to do. This is how I always pictured my summer vacation.

Minutes later she turns around, and says, "How come you're not riding your bike anymore? I don't think I ever remember seeing you around without your bike."

Sometimes I wish she wouldn't talk. I was just getting over thinking about my bike, and had convinced myself I needed a new one anyway. But now I'm feeling sick to my stomach all over again remembering how Owen Scaggs simply took it. I put my hand to my head and begin rubbing my temples. I mumble, "I lost it."

"How in the world did you lose your bike?"

I've nothing to lose by letting her in on it. "Don't tell anyone, but do you know that dirtbag Owen Scaggs? He took it from me."

Her eyes widen, and her expression is disbelieving as she sits down next to me on the couch. "Seriously?"

"Yep."

"How did it happen?"

I close my eyes. "Do you really need to know?"

"Of course I need to know," she says. "I'm your friend, aren't I?" She looks at me with concern.

"Well," I hesitate. "I was riding home from here and it got dark. I was going up the big hill just before Main Street when he sort of jumped out of the dark and took it. Now it's his."

"Just like that, you let him take it from you?"

"Just like that," I said. "Nobody messes with Owen Scaggs.

You know he was sent to juvenile prison, and everyone says it was for stabbing some kid with a knife?"

"You don't know that's true," she says. "For all anyone really knows he went away to summer camp."

"Well, I wasn't about to find out for myself. Besides I was thinking of getting a new bike."

"You were not thinking about getting a new bike." For the first time, she doesn't try to ask me any more questions about it, and just lets it be.

Once again we're both silent, and it's kinda nice hanging out with her even though we aren't saying much. Finally I break the silence with my own question. "Why'd you want to see my hideout so bad?"

"I don't know," she says, looking around. "A hideout sounded kind of cool. It's a lot better than hanging out at my house after school, especially because my sister Elisabeth usually brings a bunch of friends over to smoke in the basement. I can't stand the smell of cigarette smoke, and my mom pretends not to notice. I don't know why she pretends they aren't smoking."

"Maybe she really doesn't know," I offer.

"No, she knows. She's just more interested in watching her TV programs than yelling at my sister." Sara pauses for a moment, staring hard out the window, then runs a hand through her hair. "She actually isn't my real mom; she's my step-mom. My real mom died when I was little."

She looks at me, but I don't know what to say. There seems to be a little quiver in her face, but she attempts a weak smile. I'm not too sure I should ask her because I don't want to make her cry.

"My dad tells me she died in a car wreck. I don't know too much about it. But I don't want to know much about it; not yet, anyway. Maybe someday." While picking imaginary lint off her jeans, she's gazing down at the floor like she'd just stubbed her toe, but is pretending it doesn't hurt.

Changing the subject she smiles a little, and says, "So, Fisher Shoemaker, why do you like building forts? I'm sorry . . . hide . . . outs." A smirk grows on her face as if forts are for little kids, and hideouts are for gangsters.

"No real reason," I answer. "It's just something to do." That seems to satisfy her, at least for the moment.

"So, tell me a dark secret about yourself," she asks.

I wonder; do all girls ask this many questions? Because if they do, I'm going to avoid them as long as I can. Just to keep her quiet, I make something up.

"Last winter, when I was in Webster's Drugstore, I was buying some Milk Duds and when I got to the register the lady had to run to the back for a second. The thing is, she left the cash draw open. I made sure no one was looking and I grabbed a twenty dollar bill and shoved it in my pocket before she got back."

Sara looks at me; I notice she has brown eyes. A grin grows across her face, like she thinks I've done something really cool. Then, without warning, she gives my shoulder a hard shove and says, "You did NOT! You are such a liar."

"I don't have any dark secrets, are you happy?"

"What about your dad? Do you get along with him?"

"Sure," I say. "I get along with him okay. He keeps telling me I'm lazy, though, and I get tired of hearing that."

"Are you?"

"Am I lazy?" I make a sweeping gesture with my hands around the hideout. "I built all this, didn't I?" I pause, then say, "I think he says that because when he gives me chores, they aren't that much fun, so I usually find something better to do. Then he gets mad because they aren't done and calls me lazy. I don't think I'm lazy; I'd just rather have fun, that's all."

"Why? What kinds of horrible things does he ask you to do?" she asks in a mocking tone.

"Oh, I don't know. The usual stuff; cut the lawn, take the trash out."

"That doesn't sound so hard," Sara says.

The daylight is beginning to fade, and in the distance the islands are starting to shadow. The lobster boats resting on their moorings glow orange from the setting sun.

"We should be going soon or we'll be late for dinner," I say, glancing at my watch.

"This is so pretty watching the sunset from here," she says, smiling. "We can go in a few minutes. So you're a little late for dinner, big deal. My mom probably won't even notice that I'm not there."

I don't disagree, so we watch the sky turn dim as the islands evaporate into the dark with the rest of the world. There're lighted dots of red and green from the running lights of boats. The seagulls have grown quiet for the day.

"So. Is there anyone at school you like?" Sara asks, breaking the silence. When she turns to look at me, the expression on her face puzzles me.

"I don't know," I answer. "I guess I like hanging out with Johnny Binder. He's kind of funny." Sara rolls her eyes and shakes her head.

"That's not what I mean," she gives me a soft poke with her finger. "I mean are there any girls at school you like. You know . . . do you have a crush on anyone?"

Why do girls always want to know stuff like that? Of course I don't have a crush on anyone because they're always asking dumb questions like this.

Before I realize what's happening, Sara leans over, putting her lips to mine. What in the world? I pull away quickly. "What WAS that?" I gasp.

Still smiling, she says, "What, you didn't like it?"

I have no idea. My brain's on overload. "I guess it was okay. But . ...?"

"But what?" she says, and leans over to kiss me again.

This time I don't pull away. She's all over me.

Finally she stops to catch her breath and says, "That wasn't so bad, was it?"

My mind's spinning a hundred miles per hour, and I'm not even sure I hear her talking. It was sort of tingly and her lips were kind of soft. Was I doing it right? This time I lean in to kiss her back and she doesn't stop me.

I honestly have no idea how long we've been on the old sofa making out, but in the dark I look down at the little glowing hands on my watch.

"Holy crap! I'm in huge trouble! I'm so late for dinner my dad is going to kill me. We gotta get going!" I grab Sara's hand, yanking her up from the sofa and make for the door. It's pitch black outside but I still know the route like the back of my hand.

"Slow down," she says. "You're not going to be in any less trouble if you get back ten minutes sooner."

She's right; my dad's not going to be any less mad if I get home ten minutes sooner. I give her hand a soft squeeze and slow down to enjoy the walk home with Sara.

With all the wonderful things that've just happened, as we

walk hand in hand, my mind begins to wander. Now it seems my hideout suddenly has a whole new purpose, one that I would never have thought of; it's now a make-out place. Also, I feel like I'm instantly much older than all my friends because I've just made out. It's funny how fast things can change.

« Chapter 5 »
The Body

Walking to her house, I'm happily holding Sara's hand. I've never thought being with a girl would be like this. In fact, most of the time I try to keep as far away as possible from girls. But the funny thing is, at the same time, I hope and pray no one will see us. Me and Sara Banks holding hands; if my friends ever found out, it would be all over school. I don't know if I'd like that or not. I keep telling myself to let go of her hand, but I just don't want to.

When we get to her driveway I'm a little disappointed that it's over for the night. What a night! Then, as if we had been doing this all summer, she turns and gives me one last kiss. "See you tomorrow," she says, smiling, and then turns and walks to the front door.

"Mmuhm," I mumble. I just stand there, watching her head toward the house, and finally think to give her a slight wave. She smiles again. My mind's fuzzy and my world's spinning. It's a good spin. I think. And I can't wait for the next time I can kiss her. Maybe tomorrow?

The door closes behind her, snapping me out of my daze, when suddenly I realize how late I am. When I get home my dad will. without a doubt, punish me big-time. Oh yeah, this is bad. Really bad.

I take off, sprinting. Sara's house is on the other side of Trent Harbor . . . just my luck. I have a long way to go. There're a couple of good shortcuts that lead through a few backyards, and across the back parking lot of a liquor store. In one yard, I stop at the fence to have a quick look to make sure the owner of the house isn't outside, then I let myself in through the gate. I take off sprinting again, across the yard to the side of the hedge, dive through a gap, and roll out on the next street over. THWAPP! I take a branch in the face. It hurts, but it saved five minutes.

Even though I might be grounded for weeks, it was still worth it. I can't stop thinking about the kiss, and the way her lips felt on mine. I'm starting to realize why a lot of the older guys are always talking about chicks.

I'm starting to get tired, so I slow to a jog. I can feel my shirt getting damp with sweat. Up ahead is Jerry's Liquor, where a trail from behind the dumpster in the back parking lot leads all the way to three streets over. It'll save a lot of time.

Just before I get to the liquor store, a strange feeling comes over me. My back begins to tingle, like an ice cube just ran along my spine. I don't think it's from all the sweating. What's with that? But I don't have any time to waste on strange feelings. I keep going, then I head around to the back of the store.

In the back lot, an older maroon-colored Buick sits parked by itself as I round the corner. The trunk is open and standing next to the car is Trent Harbor's chief of police, Officer O'Reilly. I chuckle to myself because my imagination always gets the best of me. I'm just being weird about the strange feeling.

Officer O'Reilly is easy to recognize, even in the poor light. His huge frame has a certain amount of authority to it and, because of this, people don't mess with him. For the most part, though, he's one of the friendliest guys in town. His hair is always clipped short in a military cut and, unlike the big droopy mustaches everyone else is wearing, his is always trim and neat.

Most people in town know Officer O'Reilly and just call him by his first name—Eddie. I know him because he comes to our school every year to talk on Bike Safety Day, and again on Career Day. Whether he's down by the docks or patrolling the streets, he always stops for a friendly chat. Everyone in town thinks he's the greatest.

As I approach, I realize Mayor Reed is standing next to him. I don't know the mayor personally, and have only heard people talk about him. Usually it's good things.

I shoot them a friendly wave and call out a hello. Suddenly, both stop what they're doing and look at me in alarm. I stop. I'm not sure what I've done.

Then I see it. Near the open trunk, next to the Mayor, is a

large cloth sack. The lumps inside the sack are shaped like a body. Holy crap, a body! What the hell are they doing with a body? My legs will not move. I'm frozen. I probably shouldn't have seen what I just saw. Was it really a body? Terror strikes me like an explosion.

The three of us—the chief, the mayor, and me—gawk at each other in absolute disbelief. Time stops dead still. What's probably only a fraction of a second feels like an hour.

"Hey, Fisher," Officer O'Reilly calls out as he fumbles with the sack, trying to hide it from my view. "What are you doing out so late?"

"Uh, nothing much," I answer, backing slowly away from the scene that is still registering in my brain. "Late for dinner, that's all."

"Well, the mayor and I could give you a ride home, if you like," he says, glancing sideways at Mayor Reed with a "just go along with it" kind of look.

"Um, no thanks, I…I don't want to interrupt," I stutter.

"Aw, no problem, in fact, I think it would be a really good idea if we did give you a ride home, Fisher, so we could have a little talk, you know?"

That's all it takes! My legs abruptly take charge of my brain, and I dash for the opening to the shortcut behind the dumpster. I've never moved so fast in my life.

"Fisher!" Officer O'Reilly suddenly cries out.

Behind me I can hear two sets of feet hitting the pavement. For a big man, I wouldn't have expected Officer O'Reilly to move very fast, but he's gaining on me.

The opening's just feet away, so I throw in an extra burst of speed. The gap's nothing more than two of the lower boards missing from the bottom of the fence, and even for me it's going to be a squeeze. Without a second to spare, I dive for it, wiggling through. But just as I pull my foot through, I can feel O'Reilly's powerful hand on my shoe. As I roll away from the fence he isn't able to keep a grip. Now out of his reach, I sprint down the dark path, desperately trying to think what I should do next.

The dark path is like some crazy tunnel of terror; branches slap my face, and roots attack my feet, yet I feel none of it. I can't suck enough air into my lungs. It's like trying to breathe water. I'm flying in a dream. But the dream's real. I think about nothing else but getting away. That's all that matters. I saw something I shouldn't have.

At the other end of the trail, I've popped out on Hope Street, several blocks away from the Buick. There's no quick way for them to get where I am now. They'll have to drive around. I don't have much time to get out of open sight. And I need a plan.

Suddenly everything seems quiet, and I try hard to get my breathing under control so I can listen for any cars or footsteps. I hear nothing. The silence starts to scare me.

45

I remember there's a really cool tree fort in the next yard over. Being a fort builder myself, when I first saw it, I liked how high it was off the ground. No one would ever notice a fort up there. I sprint for the ladder on the back side of the tree, then scramble up as fast as I can. My hands fly from rung to rung.

I have a little luck; the trap door's not locked and I easily flip it open. I quickly climb through, trying not to make any noise, then shut the door back into place. There's a sliding bolt lock on the inside so I secure it, making sure it'll hold.

It's quiet again except for the noise of my heart beating in my chest and making its way to my skull. I swear if anyone was standing below, they'd be able to hear the pounding, but I keep telling myself that's impossible.

When my heart stops racing, the every day sounds of the neighborhood become magnified. It's as if my hearing has become super sensitive. I listen for anything that might sound like a car engine . . . especially a Buick with a big V-8.

Minutes pass. Before I know it, a glance at my watch tells me a half hour has gone by.

Sitting in the dark silence, my mind begins to spin out of control. Did I really see a body being loaded into the trunk? It could have been a sack of potatoes. After all, my crazy imagination has gotten me in trouble before. There's that time at summer camp I was certain our cabin was haunted. I was so scared, I wouldn't even get up at night to take a pee. I ended up wetting the bed. I had to wake up early before everyone else so I could change the sheets, or face being teased for the rest of the session. It turns out what I thought were ghosts were only noisy squirrels in the walls.

Is this my imagination again? Did I really see what I thought I saw—the police chief and the mayor stuffing a dead body into a car? That just can't be right. But why else would they chase me? Maybe I should just come down out of the tree and find out what they really want.

My gut jumps into my throat when I hear the sound of a vehicle approaching from off in the distance. I'm holding my breath, listening as it becomes louder. Just as the car passes under the tree fort it stops, then idles beneath me. It could be a Buick, but I can't be sure. I hold my breath.

I listen closely, but hearing anything is hard over the pounding heartbeat that fills my ears once again. I close my eyes. A car door squeaks open. Then another. Two men are talking in low voices.

"This is where the path comes out," one of them says. I can just barely make out the voice as Officer O'Reilly's.

Please don't look up, please don't look up.

The mayor says, in a whisper, "We need to find that Shoemaker boy. If he talks and anyone finds out about this, there'll be hell to pay."

47

I slap my hands over my mouth to keep from screaming out!

"I know where his family lives," the police chief says. "After we get rid of the car, I'll go over and have a look around. Maybe we'll get lucky and he'll be hiding out in the yard or something. Who knows, maybe I just go to the door and tell his dad I need to ask him some questions."

That's all I need to hear! I'm convinced now, this is not my crazy imagination. I need a plan, and I need to come up with it fast. I certainly can't go home, because that's the first place they plan to look. I'm going to have to go to my hideout. I'd never have dreamed I'd actually need my hideout. . . to hide out.

By the time the two car doors close, and the sound of the engine disappears into the night, it feels like hours. I slowly count to one hundred before I leave the safety of the tree fort.

But first I listen hard again, just one last time to be sure. Nothing. It's safe.

I slowly slide the lock across and carefully open the trap door, knowing if I make any kind of sound it'll be the end of me. I start to shake. Taking a deep breath, I try my best to calm down. I've never been this scared before. I poke my head out through the trap door opening and have a quick look around; all clear. Down the ladder I climb. Once on the ground I flatten myself up tight against the tree so no one can see me as I take a quick look around. All clear again.

So as not to attract attention to myself, I reason, I should walk slowly right out in the open rather than run. I slide out from behind the tree as if I'm just out for a nice summer evening stroll. My gut is screaming RUN, but my brain overrules while I continue my walk as if I don't have a care in the world. I have a LOT to care about, though; my life!

There's one other thing I need to do first before sneaking out to my hideout: I have to keep my parents from looking for me. I need to make a call.

At the end of the block is a gas station, closed down for the night, with a phone booth on the side. Perfect. Inside the booth there's a collection of bugs swarming around the light, and dead bugs everywhere. I brush a few of them away while fishing around in my pockets for a nickel. Quickly, I drop it into the slot and dial my house number.

My sister answers the phone, and she's quick to inform me that I'm in big trouble for missing dinner. "Dad is going to skin you alive," she says, happily.

"Just put Mom on the phone," I say, in a cold tone that means business. There's a pause.

Mom picks up, "Fisher where are you? You've missed dinner."

"Yeah, I know. I'm at John Blackwell's house. His mom

invited me for dinner so I—"

"You know you should have called," my mom interrupts, "we had no idea where you were."

"Sorry," I apologize. "I'm going to stay the night, it's okay with his mom."

She quickly answers, "On a weeknight? Oh, no . . ."

Damn! I hadn't thought of that! In my mom's eyes, overnights are only for the weekend, even if it is summer vacation. Quickly I do the old "bad connection" trick by rubbing the receiver on my shirt sleeve to make a static noise, and then I hang up fast. I hope she doesn't call back John Blackwell's house. I'm in the clear... maybe. But if it worked, that'll only hold them over for a day.

I don't want to be in the light of the phone booth any longer than I need to be so, again, I make for the shadow of the side street next to the gas station.

The town is unusually quiet, and the silence is deafening.

Now I need to let Sara know I'm in a jam because I know I'm going to need her help; I just don't know how yet. Looking back at the phone booth gives me an idea.

I don't have paper or a pen with me, but the phone booth has both. A written message to Sara should do the trick.

Even though the phone book paper is yellow, and full of print, there's plenty of it. I go back to the booth and tear a page out to write my message. But then, somehow, I'm going to need to get it to her. In the movies, they always toss stuff through the bedroom window. The problem is, I don't have any idea where her bedroom window's located. This idea suddenly stinks.

Then it hits me. What a dumb kid I am. I put my hand into my pocket and fish around for another nickel. I open the phone book and look up the Banks residence. Then, with the pen, I circle their phone number.

The phone rings three times before Sara's mom answers it.

"Hello," I say. "Can I speak with Sara, please?"

"Can I ask who's calling? She's not allowed to take calls from boys so late." Her tone is not friendly at all. I'm glad I'm not standing in front of her at the moment, asking to see Sara.

"This is Fisher Shoemaker. I need to talk to her about a homework assignment." School has actually been out for about a week now, but this seems to work. The phone's quiet for a minute while Sara comes to pick up.

"Fisher?" says the girl's voice on the other end. "Hey, I'm so glad you called. I was just thinking about tonight, and—"

"I can't talk right now," I say, cutting her off. "I need you to meet me at the hideout tomorrow afternoon. I've got a big problem, but I can't tell you just yet. I have to go." Quickly, I hang up the phone. I've been in the lighted phone booth way too long, and I need to get back to the shadows of the dark.

51

∞ ∞ ∞

Soon I'm at the end of the abandoned road. I've been there so many times that finding it in the dark isn't difficult. When I finally get inside with the door shut, the first thing I do is flop down on the old sofa. The fear and adrenalin that has consumed me all night begins to settle down, and the dangerous situation I'm now in becomes a little clearer in my head.

The whole scene replays in my head; it all happened so fast. I don't really remember much of anything after Sara kissed me good night. But then I was suddenly standing, frozen with fear, in the parking lot as the police chief and mayor were shoving a body into the trunk of a car. After that, everything seemed to accelerate at the speed of light; and here I am.

Looking around, I realize that as well as this place is hidden, it'll only be a matter of time before someone finds me. I sure don't want to find out what'll happen to me when they do. And, of course, the police chief will be the first person I'll face. Also, by tomorrow night, when I still haven't come home, my parents will realize something is wrong and call the police.

In small towns like Trent Harbor, people always rally together when there's a problem. There'll probably be a massive search, with the neighbors volunteering just like they did when that kid went missing last summer. When they found him, he was sleeping under a picnic table in the park. If that happens, the townspeople would be putting me right in the hands of two killers. It might be a day or two, but surely they'd find me here. I need a better plan.

The day's events have worn me out more than I thought because, no matter how hard I try to concentrate on a plan, sleep overtakes me.

∞ ∞ ∞

Blinking hard several times, because there's crust in the corner of my eyes, things slowly come into focus. Somehow morning has arrived. Some of the distant islands just past the harbor are coming into view as the light from the rising sun makes them glow. There're several seagulls fighting over a clam. I look around to see that I'm still in my hideout on the sofa.

Thoughts inside my head move slowly, like thick, sticky molasses, and the events from last night seem unreal. But slowly, all the crazy things begin to become clear. It is all real; I am still in a life-or-death situation.

The sun continues to climb. The trees on the distant islands become greener, and the sea turns from a steel gray to a deep cool blue. I watch intently. I notice how the different angles of sunlight can change the look of everything. As the sea spray hits the rocks and shoots upward, it seems whiter and frothier than ever before.

Also, there's a cormorant drifting about, occasionally diving for its morning meal of fish.

I stand up and look out at the islands, my gaze narrowing in concentration. Suddenly, my plan is crystal clear.

« CHAPTER 6 »

Escape by Sea

The night on the sofa was long and restless. My mind was heavy with fear. At some point, between all the tossing and turning, I must've fallen asleep. But the way I feel right now, it sure doesn't seem like it. My brain feels like hardening cement.

Now that it's daylight, probably the best thing to do is to just stay put for the day. If I step outside someone might see me. I can't take that chance.

So I spend most of the day right here on the sofa where, the night before, Sara Banks kissed me. I can't even enjoy the memory anymore, though, because I'm thinking so hard about what I need to do next. This whole situation is just so crazy!

My stomach groans. Hunger's the one thing I hadn't counted on. The empty feeling in my belly is painful, and I feel like could eat the leg off the table. There're some wild blueberries along the roadside, but considering what might happen to me if I'm caught, I think I'll stay in the hideout, where it's safe. I can deal with the hunger no matter how bad it gets.

Thinking about food reminds me that this is Friday. I'm supposed to start my restaurant job tonight. I have to admit, the extra money would have been nice. I was already starting to think about the things I was going to do with it. First, I was going to buy a new bike. Without a job, it what would have taken most of the summer to save up the money. Then I was thinking it would be cool to buy a stereo system. It would have the big speakers, as big as two milk crates stacked on top of each other, and the music would shake the house. For sure, it would drive my dad nuts, but I wouldn't have cared; it would've been my money. I could do what I wanted with it. The cool thing would be being the only kid in school with his own stereo system.

I dream some more about the money I'm not going to have.

I realize skipping my first day of work is only going to get me in even more hot water. Mrs. Fennel's going to be upset, and my dad isn't going to like it one bit. Everyone's going to be mad at me, but they're just going to have to take a number and get in line. My life is in danger. I'm sticking with my plan. There's no other way.

The last hour before Sara arrives is the longest. I'm excited to see her. I want to get going with my plan and, of course, I'm starving. I sure hope she brings some food.

I hear footsteps coming down the path. Knowing it's probably Sara I still freeze in one place because I can't be sure. Careful not to make a sound, I grab hold of the rope that leads to the crate of rocks above the door.

There's a light tap. "Fisher, it's me, Sara," says the voice on the other side.

I open it a crack to peek through. There she is, brown hair hanging loose, and dressed in clothes that, once again, do not look like her sister's old hand-me-downs. I notice she's carrying her small sailing duffel bag, so she must have just come from afternoon sailing class. Ah, Sara. I'm happier to see her than I ever thought possible. I open the door to let her in, and then quickly close it behind her.

Not really sure if it's the right thing to do, or not, I lean in any way to give her a kiss. She stops me cold by putting her hand up in front of my face.

"Whoa, wait a minute, mister. You can't be doing that because I need to know what the heck is going on." I feel stupid, hanging in midair, waiting for a kiss.

"Well," I say, wondering just how much I should tell her for her own safety. "It's like this. Last night, when I was walking home from your house, I saw something that I shouldn't have and now I need to get out of here."

"What did you see?" Her arms are crossed, and she has a serious look about her.

I take a deep breath. "Something really bad, so bad that I need to get out of here."

"Tell me," Sara insists.

For her own safety, I shouldn't tell her any more than she needs to know. But on the other hand, she could be a big help getting me out of this jam. I reason she's a smart girl; I'm sure she'll be careful.

I hesitate, then say, "I saw Police Chief O'Reilly and the mayor shoving a dead body into the trunk of a car."

She listens intently to the words I'm saying, and then a smile grows across her face. "You did not! You are just saying that to get me here to your hideout, and—"

I slam my fist down hard on the table, surprising myself more than her. "It's true! They saw me, and now they're looking for me. If they catch me, I could be the next one in the trunk. I think I'm in an awful lot of trouble."

"You're serious," she says, putting both hands to her face. "But why would they do such a thing?"

"How should I know? Whatever the reason, I need to stay hidden until this clears over."

We sit down on the sofa and I take her hand in mine while I tell her the whole story of what happened. She doesn't say anything, or ask any questions, until I'm done.

Her face is pale, and her eyes have a faraway look. Finally, she says, "This is bad, really bad."

"I know. I've been thinking about this all day. The only thing I can think of is I need to get out of here; at least for a little while until things cool down a bit."

"What do you mean you have to get out of here? Where will

you go?"

"I have to leave Trent Harbor."

"You're serious," she says. "Why don't you just tell your dad what you saw? I'm sure he'll know what to do."

"I can't. I overheard police Chief O'Reilly last night and they're watching my house. They'll grab me the second I get near."

"But you can't just run away. If you don't come home, your parents are going to go to the police anyway."

"I don't know what else to do. I'm scared out of my mind," I say, closing my eyes. I wish this would all just go away. "If I stay here, I'm sure as dead. And, if I leave here, my dad is going to kill me anyway. I'm only thirteen; I don't have too many choices."

"But your mom is going to be worried sick about you."

"I can't help it. I feel terrible about it."

I just shake my head. Finally, I say, "There're hundreds of islands out there. I'm just going to sail to one and stay there for a while."

"That's a bad plan," she says, with a little quiver in her voice. "Where are you going to get a sailboat? Did you think about that?"

"Are you kidding me? I've had all day to think about it," I say, getting a little irritated at the question. I'm edgy, though. "Do you know the summer home at the end of Lark Street? With the statue of the eagle out front? Well, those people never come up here until August. But their sailboat's already in the water and docked on the pier outside their house. It's the perfect size for me, about 21 feet with a cutty cabin. I can singlehand it, no problem."

"You can't just sail away in a boat that's not yours! That's stealing! Besides, someone is going to see you in it and they'll tell the harbor master. You'll be picked up and sitting in the police station in a matter of hours. And you can add boat theft to your list of problems."

"That's why I'm going to leave after dark," I say, adding, "The tide will be high about then, and I'm sure as hell not going to turn on the running lights."

"You're crazy! Do you know how many rocks are out there for you to run into?"

She doesn't need to remind me; anyone who lives in Maine knows there are hundreds of smashed up boats that have hit rocks. Some made it back to shore and others sank. If you don't know the area it's dangerous to go out there in a boat, even in daylight. Just the tide and crazy currents alone can mess up even the best local lobsterman. Knowing the waters only makes it a little less dangerous.

Her angry expression clearly shows she does not like this idea, but I really have no choice.

"Look, I'll be fine," I say to try and reassure her, but I'm not even convincing myself.

"Here's what I need you to do. I need you to go and get

some food, as much as you can carry, and meet me at 9 o'clock tonight at the boat. Can you do that?"

She looks scared, but nods her head yes. "Try to get canned foods and things that won't spoil."

Talking about food quickly reminds me that I'm starved. "Do you have anything to eat right now?" I ask. Sara reaches into her duffel bag and hands over a half-eaten sandwich. Wow. I never thought a bologna and cheese sandwich would taste so good. It's gone in two bites.

Watching me inhale her sandwich, she says, "What are you going to tell your parents? Don't you think they're going to make a big scene when you don't come home?"

It's true; they're probably going to send out a search party for me. Any parent would. I think hard about it. I'll have to give them some sort of letter to reassure them I'm okay so they won't come looking for me. An idea tickling the back of my mind begins to take shape.

When my dad was about my age, he left home to take a job with the Civilian Conservation Corps. He's always talking about it, but I never paid too much attention. I sort of remember that the CCC built hiking trails and made things for parks during the Depression. It was like big work camps for young men or something like that. I also remember he said he lied about his age because he was only thirteen, and they only recruited boys that were seventeen

61

and older. But it's one of those things in his life he was proud of; he was earning money for his family during the Depression. Maybe that's why he's always riding me about working hard and not being lazy.

"Do you have a pen and paper?" I ask Sara. She pulls a piece of paper out of her three-ring binder and hands me a pen.

I write, *Dear Mom and Dad*, but that's as far as I get. I think hard about what I'm going to write because it has to keep them from looking for me, or worrying. I wipe my sweaty palms on my jeans and look at what I've written, hoping for inspiration: *Dear Mom and Dad*, but my mind goes blank. I take a deep breath, and try it again.

Dear Mom and Dad,

Please do not be upset with me, but listening to Dad's stories about how he worked in the CCC building trails and parks made me think I should try the same thing. I am going to take the bus to Vermont and see if I can get a job working at one of the parks. I have some money from my savings account, so I should be okay for a while. Please do not worry; Dad did this when HE was my age and everything turned out OK. I will send you a letter as soon as I can when I find a job at a park, or whoever will take me.

Love, your son,
Fisher

I'm not totally convinced the letter will work, but that's all I can come up with. If nothing else, maybe it'll send them in the wrong direction, but I truly do not want them to worry about me. I fold it up and hand it to Sara.

"Can you make sure they get this? Do not tell them anything. It might be best if you just leave it at the front door for them to find so they don't start asking you questions. If they figure out you dropped it off, tell them you only know what's in the letter, but nothing else. Got it? Oh, and don't drop it off until after I've left. If they start looking for me I want to make sure I'm long gone."

She nods, also not totally convinced that this will work.

I add, "I think you should get going. You've got to get some food for me and I need to leave on the high tide. The longer I wait, the better my chances are at hitting a rock."

"But Fisher," Sara protests. "Are you sure this is a smart thing to do?"

"I don't think it's smart at all, but I don't think I have any other choice."

I stand up, pulling her with me, and look into her eyes. "I'll be fine." But I don't really believe it myself. "Get going."

At the door she turns to look at me, then quickly closes it behind her. Suddenly, I'm alone again. I better get used to being alone.

I have a plan in front of me that makes me feel a little

better, but there're just so many things happening so fast. I flop
back down on the sofa, squeezing my eyes tight.

If I wasn't late last night, I wouldn't have taken that shortcut
through the back parking lot of the liquor store, and I wouldn't have
seen the police chief and mayor shoving a body into the trunk. Why
do things like that happen? It could've been anybody, but it was me.
Now I have a huge problem.

As time passes and the daylight begins to fade, I start to get
antsy. I'm feeling like there's something I need to prepare for sailing
tonight. If I was just heading out on a day sailing trip there'd still be
lots of things I needed to do; pack a lunch, gather foul-weather gear,
and check the weather report. But waiting here, in my hideout, with
nothing but the clothes on my back, leaves me feeling a little sick to
my stomach.

Added to that, I'm not even sure I know where I'm going,
and what islands I can actually land on. I've never looked at a chart
much past our own harbor. Once, in our sailing classes, we were
taught how to read a chart and walk off miles with dividers, but that
was only one rainy afternoon about a year ago. We never had a
chance to try it for real. I should've asked Sara to grab a chart from
the sailing club. Damn! Now I think of the good ideas!

After what feels like an eternity, my watch says 8 o'clock. It's
dark outside, and time to go. I look around the place. I have no
things to collect, so I just leave.

I wonder if I'm ever going to see this place again. It feels like I'll be back tomorrow, just like always, but I know it'll be a long time before I'll be coming back. I hope it'll still be here when I return. Walking quickly, I leave the hideout behind me in the darkness.

Getting to the house on Lark Street is taking me much longer than I planned. I need to stay hidden in the shadows of the dark as much as I can. In some places I take side streets with no streetlights, and that takes longer, too.

The house with the eagle in front is like most of the summer homes in Maine. It's big, with lots of bedrooms, so a mess of family members can all stay for one big gathering. Also, it has a huge porch that wraps around the whole house with lots of chairs overlooking the ocean. People who own houses like this one are usually from someplace else because most people from Trent Harbor can't afford a place like this.

Behind the house is a path that leads down to the water where the owner has a private dock with a larger power boat and a sailboat tied off. Soon to be *my* sailboat.

When I get down to the dock it's dark and quiet, with no one around. I study the boat and hope I'll be able to sail it by myself. This one, being a little bigger than the club boats I'm used to, usually needs one other person to act as crew to help trim the sails and such. By myself, I'm going to have my hands full.

The wooden planks on the hull are painted a bright white with a small blue cove strip just under the rail. Even in the dark the boat looks stunning. Each piece of mahogany trim is perfectly varnished and the shine off the trim, even in the low light, makes it look wet. The boatyard that delivered it to the dock has coiled up each line and sheet in a perfect little circle, making everything as neat and tidy as they could. This customer must be a good one because they made sure everything is just so. I feel bad that whenever the day comes when the owner arrives, the guys at the boatyard are going to get the blame for the missing sailboat.

I notice just before I climb aboard that there's a gentle breeze out of the west, which is almost perfect for sailing out of the harbor. With no motor on the boat, I'm going to have to use all my skills to sail it out of the harbor. A westerly breeze should let me sail in a straight line and not have to worry about tacking back and forth. That makes me feel a little better.

In the dark, I'm careful stepping on board. There're plenty of things to trip on. Taking a look at the deck, I try to memorize where everything is laid out. Sailing solo I'll be busy enough without having to figure out where everything is in the dark so, the more I know, the better off I'll be. Satisfied I know what's what, I go below.

It's totally dark down here, but I need to find some charts. Somehow fumbling around the galley, I feel my way toward the stern and manage to stumble across a box of matches, so I strike one, which reveals two oil lamps. Perfect. I only light one up because I'm afraid someone might see light coming out of the porthole.

But soon there're footsteps coming down the dock, so I quickly reach over and snuff out the oil light. Please let it be Sara, I think. If it's anyone else, I'm done for. There're two short steps that lead out of the cabin to the cockpit, so I step on the bottom one and cautiously poke my head out to see. It's hard to tell in the dark. All I can make out is the silhouette of a person carrying a small bundle.

Standing almost over me, on the dock, Sara says, in a soft voice, "Fisher?"

"I'm down here," I call up to her.

I still really can't see her face in the dark, but I suddenly feel a little less nervous about what I'm about to do. If it all goes wrong, this is going to make for great town gossip: *Did you hear about that boy who stole a sailboat and smashed it up on the rocks?*

She's particularly careful not to make any noise as she climbs aboard, then hands me the sack.

In a whisper, she says, "It's mostly canned stuff I found in my mother's pantry. None of it's all that good, but it's the best I could do. There's squash, beans, and soup. Oh, and I found a loaf of bread, too."

"That's great," I say, trying to reassure her. "Help me get the sails up. Then I'm going to need you to give me a shove off the dock."

In the dark, we make our way topside and unfurl the sails.

After the sails are hanked on, we both pull hard on the halyard. When the mainsail begins to go up, a light breeze catches it and it starts to luff back and forth, making clanging noises from the metal fittings slapping about. I might as well start ringing church bells for all the noise we're making.

"Hurry!" I say, in a loud whisper. Both of us pull even harder on the halyard. Next, we grab the jib and do the same thing. From the slapping of both sails there is just too much noise in the otherwise quiet night. I need to get out of here!

Once the sails are up and I'm satisfied how they look, I grab Sara's hands and say, "I've got to go now before someone hears us."

I give her a kiss, and this time it seems even better than I remembered it.

Then I say, "Somehow I'll get a message to you that I'm all right. I don't know how, but I'll think of something."

She throws the lines off and gives the bow a hard shove with her foot, sending me off into the current while I harden up on the sails. When the sails are tight, the loud racket from the luffing comes to a stop. It's almost silent now except for the water rushing past the hull, which only leaves a foamy trail.

It seems funny now; I'd been so careful to remember my compass heading, but now it's absolutely useless because I can't read any of the numbers on the compass in the dark. Another trick I remember reading about is to find a light from the town behind me and make sure it stays in the same place over the transom the whole time. If I can keep the light in the same spot, it means I'm sailing in a straight line. But that only works if I'm going in the right direction in the first place; all I can do is hope I am.

The boat handles well, even better than I thought it would. I let out a deep breath and begin to relax a little and just concentrate on keeping it going in a straight line. Straining my eyes as hard as I can doesn't seem to help to see things in the dark, but the farther away I get from the lights on shore, the more my eyes adjust to the darkness.

Suddenly, there's something black, like a large demon coming right at the bow. I pull hard on the tiller trying to miss whatever it is. BANG! Scraping sounds screech along the side of the hull. In a dreadful instant I realize I've hit another sailboat on a mooring. In the low light I couldn't see the dark green hull of the other sailboat until it was too late. Almost as quickly as I've hit it, it disappears behind me, back into the darkness like a ghost.

In a moment of complete terror I'm not sure what I should do. Go back to the dock? Go below and look for damages? Or keep going? The boat still seems to be steering well, and as far as I can tell the rigging and sails aren't damaged. I'm worried that I may have punched a hole in the side of the boat, but honestly I wasn't going that fast so chances are good all that happened was I scraped the perfect paint job. I decide to keep going.

I promise myself that if I get out of this whole thing alive, someday I'll somehow pay for a new paint job. But at the moment, all I can do is keep sailing the boat as best I can and be more careful.

Minutes turn into hours as I sail the boat in a nice straight line. The lights on shore grow smaller and the buildings that were lit up become harder to recognize. If my guess is right, I should be in open water now, away from any more hazards like boats on moorings, or worse—jagged rocks. I'm also pretty sure all the channel markers are well behind me, too.

My mind begins to wander, and I start to think about Sara standing there on the dock as I disappeared into the dark night. It was only about a week ago that I was trying to avoid her, and any other girl for that matter. But now I can't stop thinking about her. What changed? Why had she helped me when she could've just stayed home where it was safe? I shake the thought off and remind myself not to let my guard down; my life depends on this sailboat, and this sailboat depends on me.

At this point, my plan's pretty simple; just keep sailing in the same direction until daylight because I know I'm safe in the direction I'm heading. Once there's a little light I'll be able to get my bearings and figure out just where I am. Heck, once it's light I can have a look at the chart and figure out where I want to go. There're a lot of islands out there for one person to disappear into. Wherever it is I'm going, it's still a long way off.

Part II
« CHAPTER 7 »
Fog

Daylight begins to drill through my eyelids like laser beams. Suddenly I bolt upright, trying to shake the fuzz out of my brain as fast as I can. Damn! I must've fallen asleep! I pound the deck hard with my hand. Falling asleep was the wrong thing to do. It's a miracle I'm still alive and actually still sailing in a straight line. I have no idea how that happened because the boat should have veered off course which would have woken me up when the sails started clanging.

The fog in my head just does not want to let go, but I force myself to shake it off, and take in my surroundings as fast as I can.

Looking around quickly, I realize I cannot see land in *any* direction! The best I can tell is that I'm still heading out to open sea. A fast glance at the compass tells me I'm still on course in the same direction as when I left Trent Harbor.

Out in the vast open ocean also means no one can see me. I got away clean! If no one knows I'm out here, I can now sail anywhere I want. But that's also the problem.

Not being able to see land means there's no way to pick a

bearing, like a hill, a radio tower, or a city water tank. I've absolutely no idea where I am. In Maine there's always an island, peninsula, or some kind of shoreline poking into the sea . . . but not this far out.

I'm confident if I alter my course just a bit to the north I should run into something I might recognize, but I better check first. Tying off the tiller so the boat steers itself, I go below deck to have a look at the chart.

Now that there's some light and I can see everything down below, I notice how much better the inside of the tiny cabin looks. I smile. At least I hit the jackpot and made off with a decent boat. It'll make a nice little living space for the time being.

A quick sharp pain in my stomach, followed by a loud rumble, reminds me I haven't eaten since yesterday. Before digging for the chart, I quickly grab the bag of canned food Sara has put together, and I pull out a can of Ravioli-Os. I also see she's placed a Swiss Army Knife in the bag, along with a note attached to it. I carefully unfold the note.

Dear Fisher:

I figured you could use a jackknife, so I found an old one of my dad's. Hope you find it useful. Please be safe and come home soon.

Always,

Sara.

That was a good idea for her to make sure I had a jackknife. She's a good person. There's no telling what I'm going to need it for, but I'm certain on this crazy adventure it's going to be one of the more useful things. And sure enough, the first thing I do is carefully pull out the can-opener blade to cut the lid off the tin can of Ravioli-Os.

While I'm eating cold ravioli out of the can, which isn't as bad as I thought it was going to be, I unroll the chart and begin to study it in detail. With a pencil and a straight edge, I draw a line from where I left and aim it straight at 093 degrees, east being the compass course at the moment. All I can do is assume that I've sailed that direction all through the night, and I'm now somewhere along the line I have just penciled in.

Hoping my instincts are right, I figure if I start to sail north I'll come across a clump of islands where I can tuck into and drop anchor. If my wind holds, I should be able to get there before the sun goes down, but if I don't make it before sundown I'll have to heave-to for the night. I really do not want to heave-to.

Heaving-to is an old trick of stopping the boat and keeping it in one place without having to sail it, freeing the skipper to do other things. The boat just holds its place in the water as if parked. That works great in open water. But I'm not confident it'll work closer to shore, with the huge tides and currents that could carry me miles away from where I stop. I don't want to wake up stuck on a rock. I can only hope to make way to an island before sundown.

Back at the tiller, certain of where I need to go, I begin to slowly alter my course to the north where I'm sure to come across some little island that will make a decent place to hide out. Once the boat's pointed in a new course, I trim in the sails to match the wind direction.

It's still early morning with a fair breeze in the right direction, but now the dull daylight has expanded out across the water, and I can tell it's not going to be a picture post card kind of a day. The sky is sort of looking like cold gray steel. With only a T-shirt on, a little shiver is working through my body. From the looks of it, there might even be rain. That will do nothing good for my mood.

But, for the moment, my mood's actually pretty good. So far, I slipped away from town unnoticed, the sailboat's still in one piece, and I'm beginning to enjoy sailing this boat that only a few hours ago was unknown to me. I just hope I won't be in too much trouble when the day comes to return the sailboat to the owners. Hopefully everyone will understand I was running for my life.

∞ ∞ ∞

Throughout the morning, the air becomes damp with humidity. With no other clothes but the jeans and T-shirt I'm wearing, I'm beginning to get a chill. About an hour ago, just off the bow, some land had come into view but, as the air keeps getting thicker with

75

moisture, it's starting to fade from the horizon. Also, my speed's slowly dropping off because the fog's sucking out all the wind. My guess is at this pace I won't be near land for several more hours. It's only a matter of time before the Maine fog will feast on me like some big gray sea ghost.

Hours later, or so it seems, the boat hasn't moved more than a couple of yards. Visibility's gone and so is the wind. The water's now smooth, like an oil slick. The sails are drooping like damp laundry hanging out to dry. Heavy drops of moisture form on my eyelids, and when I run my hand through my hair it's almost as wet as if I'd just jumped in the water. A little shiver ripples through my body, and the visibility's now so low I can't even see the bow.

Fog is evil, and sneaky. Throughout time it's caused more mayhem to watermen than any storm. Most old timers speak of fog with a hint of fear in their voice. With a storm, a sailor usually knows it's coming and can most times make for safe waters, or at least be prepared for it. With fog, however, it just creeps in like some dangerous animal tracking its unsuspecting prey. I'm thankful the sailboat has stopped moving. If it isn't moving, it can't hit anything.

Hours pass by with no forward movement, and it's now late afternoon. I stare into the gray, but there's nothing to see. The sailboat's just sitting as if the anchor's down. With no auxiliary motor there's not much I can do, so I'm at the mercy of whatever wind, or no wind, comes my way.

∞ ∞ ∞

Thump . . . thump . . . I'm not sure I heard it at first, so I strain my ears to listen even harder. Quiet. Then, almost undetectable, I can hear it again; faint in the distance is the low sound of a diesel engine. My heart jumps into my throat. In fog this thick it's hard to tell what direction it's coming from. Fog is sneaky like that. It can carry sound in unlikely directions. For all I know, I might've been drifting in a current that pushed me closer to shore, making the noise actually a truck rumbling down a road.

But what was a faint deep rumble only a few minutes ago has gradually become a little louder so, to hear it, I no longer need to strain my ears. That's not good.

Soon the deep thumping becomes even more intense. There's no doubt that the chugging's from a diesel engine in a much larger vessel, and it's getting closer. Much closer than I like. If it's on a collision course with me, it'll never even know I'm here and will plow through the side of the hull leaving nothing more than splintered planks and a few shredded ribbons of sail. And if I'm lucky enough to survive the collision, the chance of someone actually finding me floating in the water's pretty slim. After that it wouldn't be long before the cold Maine water finished the job.

The constant deep thumping engine keeps coming closer, like a slow-moving freight train emerging from a dark tunnel.

I need to do something. Anything. Jumping down below I rummage around for anything that'll make noise; a big bell, a flair gun, anything! I need to let the oncoming vessel know there's a sailboat in its path. I'm sweating even though it's cool. As I fling open drawers, looking for anything that I can use as a signal, I notice my hands are trembling. When I find a large frying pan, I toss it on the settee and keep frantically searching other places. I'm not sure what I'm looking for, but I know from the roar of the bellowing engine there isn't much time left. Then I find a hammer; that's it! Without a second to spare, I grab the frying pan and scramble topside, landing in the cockpit.

How much louder can the engine noise possibly get without me seeing the oncoming vessel? The constant metallic thumping's now so loud that it might be right alongside. Frantically, I start banging the hammer and pan together, making a clanging noise much louder than I ever thought possible. BANG! BANG! BANG! Nothing. The other vessel hasn't heard it because it would've blasted its horn in return.

I don't stop. BANG! BANG! BANG! As hard as I can. Then, screaming at the top of my lungs, "I'm here! I'm here!" This is life or death.

Suddenly, without warning, out of the fog, all in neat rows

heading straight for the transom of my sailboat, are several mammoth sets of deadly waves. They must be the wake of the passing vessel. The cold killers on a mission to sink me look to be about ten feet high each with a steep face. When the waves strike my boat, in a flash, the transom points sharply skyward then, just as fast, drops, spraying gallons of cold water into the cockpit. The rigging and sails slap and clank hard together in noisy confusion.

Instantly dropping the frying pan and hammer, I grab the hand rail to keep from getting tossed over the side. Like some sort of wild animal trying to throw me off its back, several more times the transom rockets almost airborne, then drops, as if I'm falling off a cliff. It's all I can do to hang on!

Almost as quickly as the waves attack—they stop. I realize the diesel engine noise's now going farther away.

Whatever the vessel was, judging by the size of the wake it threw at me, it was large, and never knew it was aimed right at me. I could've easily been in a mass of broken wooden planks scattered about the frigid water. But I'm not, and I'm safe.

There'd been no time for fear. Things happened too fast. It came, it went, but now with the realization of how close I had come to being sent to the bottom, I begin shaking uncontrollably. I close my eyes tight, trying to shake it all off. I can't afford to be scared. When I open them I look around; the fog still keeps me from seeing beyond the bow pulpit. There's not much I can do but hope it doesn't happen again and, while I'm waiting out the fog to lift, get control of my emotions.

The whole scene plays and replays in my head, but I can't think of anything I could've done differently to keep the vessel from hitting me. The fog plays no favorites and it's just plain dumb luck that I'm still floating.

« CHAPTER 8 »
The Landing

Just over an hour has passed since I was almost run over. The gray murkiness still has its grip on me and, as far as I can tell, I haven't moved even a foot. But who knows, with the crazy currents in the Maine waters, I could've been pushed all the way back to Trent Harbor.

A few spots of rain begin to splatter the wood deck. I groan. I'm already cold and damp, and know if I can't stay dry it's only going to turn from bad to miserable. The drops begin to get bigger and become steadier, soaking the cockpit. Everything's a little slicker. If I'm not careful, and don't hold onto things as I move around the boat, I could slip right off the side.

Because I'm not moving, I don't need to steer. Also, in the heavy fog there's nothing to see, so I hop down below. There's no reason to sit in the rain like a confused duck.

I'm stuck down below with time to kill, so I take the opportunity to have a closer look around the small cabin. I figure it might be a good idea to take stock of what I have to work with. The cabin's tiny so it isn't going to take long. I pull open a few drawers and find all the usual things on a boat; a couple of rusty

81

screwdrivers that look older than they are, some various sizes and lengths of rope, a can opener—also rusty—and a stale jar of peanuts. Then I strike gold.

Tucked away, just behind the bulkhead, is a thin cabinet door, and hanging on a hook is a bright yellow rain slicker. I quickly put it on. The arms are way too long and I probably could have a friend in it with me, but I'm happy to have it, too big or not. Now I can sail in the rain and stay reasonably warm and dry.

It's not long before the rain really starts to pour down in buckets, but I notice that the rain seems to be knocking down the fog. The fog is starting to thin and I begin to see different shapes on the horizon that surely must be land. But there's one other thing the rain has brought back… wind.

The wind is a gift. It starts with light cat's-paws on the smooth water, and then turns into soft ripples. I can feel it on the damp skin of my face. "Whoooa Hooo!" I yell, giving the bulkhead a slap.

With the slicker hanging about me, I carefully climb out into the slick cockpit. When I was digging around before I found a short piece of rope which is now snug around my waist so the slicker isn't quite so loose. When the rain pelts the stiff yellow plastic, the noise is like being under a tin roof. Ting, ting, ting. But I can live with it as long as it keeps me dry.

The sails no longer look like wet laundry and are beginning

to show some shape. There's slightly more wind pressure. A little trail of wake begins to appear behind the boat. I'm starting to creep along. But at this rate, it's going to take days to get over toward land, yet I know this is how it always starts when more wind is about to fill in.

Sure enough, after a half hour the breeze begins to fill back in and the sailboat starts to move nicely through the water. What was gentle lapping against the hull is now the sound of rushing water. There's more heel to the boat as the sails begin to fill with greater wind power. Once again, I am on my way.

I'm still miles away from the islands I'm trying to get to. I can barely see them just off the bow. The problem is, daylight's going to fade pretty soon, and the idea of trying to get into an unknown area in the dark is terrifying. But there's no way of getting around that unless I point the bow back out to sea to wait out another night. I sure don't want to do that again. Once was enough!

When I was rummaging through the cabin earlier, I found a pair of binoculars, which are now hanging around my neck. I need to know what I'm up against.

The islands closest to me do not offer much hope. Too many rocks and big sprays of white water. I keep searching. There's one island I spot, a little farther away and just slightly to beam of me, that's not a rocky shoreline like the others. It seems to be slightly different from the darker colors of the rocks and trees. It's a sandy beach.

Dropping an anchor just off a sandy beach seems like the best idea, but that isn't always the case. On the approach there can easily be many rocks hidden beneath the water. But today, I don't have a whole lot of choices. I reason that it's a better bet the sandy area will be safer. Also, in a tight rocky cove, if the anchor moves just a little bit, even small waves could turn the boat into scrap. The cove with the sandy beach is my target.

There's only a couple of hours of daylight left, but at the speed I'm sailing, which is pretty good for this boat, it'll be close. I'd rather not have to sail in there after dark, sandy beach or not.

According to the compass, 010 degrees north is my course. The breeze is just off the port beam and I've no reason to believe it's going to change anytime soon. If I hold my course for the next hour or so it should be easy getting in.

I wish my pace was a little faster, but I'm thankful to at least be moving. Either way, for the first time since this mess started, I have some time on my hands to just relax and enjoy sailing the boat. I'm going to try hard to not think about everything that has happened.

But I do begin to think about my family. Will they even miss me? The only reason my older sister might miss me is because she'll have no one to tell on. My sister, Clair, who is bigger than me, has long dark hair, usually in a ponytail, and can't pronounce her "L's."

She also never misses an opportunity to let my dad know when I've done something wrong. Sometimes she gets me in trouble even if I haven't done something wrong.

Once when we were little, our family was headed to Portland on a long car ride to visit my cousins. I was deep into a Spider-Man comic book when suddenly my sister let out a loud yell, as if I had just punched her in the arm. But I hadn't. Without any hesitation, never taking his eyes off the road, my dad swatted at my head while yelling at me to leave my sister alone. Luckily, his aim was high. There was nothing more than a swish of air that went past my face. But that only aggravated him more. If he'd actually looked to the back seat it would've only taken him a second to figure out what she'd done; he would've seen the smirk on her face.

My mom, on the other hand, will probably be worried sick thinking I have run off to some state park a million miles away. I wonder, though: Will she be worried for my safety? Or just about some other crazy thing that doesn't matter, like maybe they won't have my favorite ice cream. She seems to miss the real problems in my life. I'll never forget the day our class had a field trip to the Maxwell lumber company. I was late, and held up the whole class because she insisted that my lunch, which I'd already put in a paper sack, be in a proper lunch box so it wouldn't get ruined. I had to wait patiently while she re-wrapped everything and repacked it into the box in her own special way. If I'd argued with her it would've made me even later because in the end, it'd still have to be done her way. I think how she might look standing by the kitchen sink. Would she be worrying about me at my park job? One part of me doesn't want her to worry, but I think secretly: I hope she does.

The mainsail suddenly makes a loud luffing noise, snapping me out of my thoughts. With a simple tug I give the mainsheet a trim, and then notice the little spot of sandy beach I'm aiming for is getting closer. Progress toward it is steady, but, unfortunately, the daylight's beginning to fade. It'll be close. Luckily the weather's calm, with the wind dropping to a light breeze, enough to keep pushing the boat ahead yet not too much to make the job of sailing by myself a handful. Even though it's becoming cool, there're small beads of sweat on my brow. I also feel like someone is squeezing my lungs. Just be cool, I tell myself. All I have to do is get in there without hitting any rocks and drop anchor. That's it.

In sailing class, we never actually practiced dropping anchor but I've a good idea what needs to happen. I go through all the steps in my head. I don't want to end up a pile of smashed planks on the rocks. Uh-oh! I never checked to see if the boat actually has an anchor. Damn! Maybe I'll be lucky and there's one sitting in the bow locker. But there's no time left to check.

At fifty yards from my target, I ease the mainsheet and let the jib flog so the momentum of the boat drops off to hardly a crawl. The luffing sails snap and chatter loudly. So far, so good. But it looks tight, and there's going to be less room to maneuver than I thought.

The second I glide over my spot I snap the bow into the wind, slowing the boat to a stop. Quickly, I jump forward to the bow locker where, I pray, the anchor is stowed. I lift the hatch and let out a sigh of relief. Thank God! There is, indeed, an anchor with rope attached. It's still clean, with no leftover mud, or rust; I don't think it's ever been used.

Not wasting a second, I grab it and heave it over the side. Splash! In it goes. I hope there's enough rope and the bottom isn't too deep. It seems to stop at what I guess is fifteen feet but, honestly, having never done this before, I wouldn't know ten feet from thirty feet. All I know is the anchor made it to the bottom with enough left over to give the boat some swing room. As I stand on the bow watching, the anchor line slowly tightens up, holding the sailboat in place like a small dog on a leash. My long day, which actually started the night before, is over. For the moment, I'm safe.

As I sit, still on the bow looking out into the dark, my jaw begins to quiver, and tears start to stream down my face. I don't know why it's happening. I'm all alone, I mean *really* alone. No one has any idea where I am and, for that matter, I actually don't know where I am, either. I'm pretty sure that people want to kill me. I'm tired. The boat, which kept me safe, is now swinging only yards away from dangerous, jagged rocks and I'm so hungry that if someone handed me a piece of cold wet seaweed I'd probably eat it. Everything that has happened today is like a wet, heavy blanket suffocating me. The tears spilling uncontrollably make me feel like a blubbering fool. But the day finally is over. At the moment, I'm safe.

« CHAPTER 9 »

Trapped

At some point I must've collapsed in my bunk from the long day and lay dead asleep. It was one of those sleeps so deep I didn't even dream. Just undisturbed darkness.

There's a far-off sound. Is it my mom cooking breakfast? Wait! I'm still in the sailboat, and the groaning noise is coming from the hull. Suddenly a force pulls me off the bunk, slamming me onto the cabin floor. This jolts me out of my deep sleep real fast. The unknown force is gravity. As I lay on the floor in my groggy state, trying to piece together what just happened, there's nothing but silence that's broken by the occasional screeching of a seagull. Bewildered, I watch helplessly as a few books from the shelf fall on me. Then it comes to me, and I have a sick feeling in my stomach; the tide has run out. The sailboat is starting to lie on its side.

"No, no, no!" I scream, fighting gravity as I try to get myself turned around. When the tide goes out there'll be no water to float the boat. In Maine, the tide can go out as much as thirteen feet, leaving a boat hard in the muddy bottom for hours.

When I dropped anchor yesterday, I'd completely forgotten about tide. We talk about it a lot at the sailing club and, living in

Trent Harbor, tide is a part of daily life that isn't much different than watching the sun rise and set. But here I am, in a little sailboat that soon will be stuck on the bottom. After that, I'll have six hours to kill until it floats again.

With every foot of water that disappears, the boat rolls over farther. Struggling out of the almost sideways hatch and sliding across the cockpit, I can see that there's only about two feet of water left. I know the idea of dropping the anchor near a sandy beach was right . . . but it's just too shallow.

Luckily, the soft, sandy bottom will gently cradle the boat, unlike rocks, which would've slowly gnawed through the wooden hull like a hungry animal. I'm fairly safe and there's nothing to worry about. I'm stuck on this island with time to kill.

For the next several hours, with the cabin now vertical, instead of horizontal, I might as well get out of here. So I pull off my shoes and jeans and drape them over my shoulders, then, in my white underwear, I hop into the knee-deep water. Man, the water is cold! After trudging to shore, I find a large rock to sit on while I pull on my pants and put my shoes back on my feet.

This island doesn't look like a place I want to stay any longer than I have to. The little area of sand where the boat lies has large rocks on both sides forming a corridor. Above the high tide mark is dense forest so thick that exploring it doesn't seem possible. Out beyond the island are several other small islands that don't look much different than the one I'm on. Way past the scattering of islands are more land formations, but it's hard to tell what's what. When the boat's floating again, I think it'll be best to keep sailing for someplace better; this just doesn't feel right.

Sitting in a dry spot in the sand with my pants back on, I consider the situation I'm in. Am I doing the right thing? How long will I have to stay away before it's safe to go back? My plan is beginning to feel a little thin, so I think harder. It could be years before it's safe to go home, but how will I really know? I halfheartedly throw a rock into the water. Will my parents believe my letter about leaving home to look for a job at a Vermont park? There're just too many questions.

I can't help thinking about my parents and my sister Clair. There's an awful sad feeling inside me making me feel miserable. Do I miss them? Do I even miss my sister who's such a pain in the butt? Maybe this is what being homesick feels like. At summer camp I had seen other kids go through it and thought they were just big wimps. My eyes begin to moisten, and I wipe them with the back of my sleeve. Big baby; I'm mad at myself for feeling this way. I am thirteen, which is too old to be homesick. I'm a complete mess.

I reach into my pocket, remembering I have the jackknife Sara gave me. Pulling it out, I turn it over in my hands, examining it. A weak smile grows across my face. With a stick I write Sara's name in the sand. It seems to make me feel better that I'm not so alone. I wonder what it would've been like if she had been here with me, a girl who recently I couldn't have cared less about.

∞ ∞ ∞

While I'm waiting for the tide to return, I peer out at all the open water I crossed yesterday in the fog. I can only guess which way Trent Harbor might be. My home. I watch two gulls floating in the calm water.

It's actually a pleasant summer day, especially for Maine. Sunny with only a few clouds, and a light breeze. This is good, seeing as I'm going to be stuck here for the next six hours. I'm very thankful that it isn't raining.

A couple of hours pass, and all the water has run out with the tide. The sailboat is now on its side in the hard sand, and resembles a wounded animal. There's no water to wade through now to get back to it.

I hoist myself into the upward angled cockpit and poke my head into the little cabin. Everything's different. The port side is now the ceiling, and the starboard side that has the bunk is now the floor. Surprisingly, most things have stayed in place. While sailboats are designed to be on their sides, they're not supposed to be this far over. There're only a few loose things now lying on the ground; books, and the rolled-up chart. Also on the floor is Sara's bag of food, which, when I see it, reminds me again that I'm hungry.

It feels like I'm *always* hungry now, but I know I have to be careful about eating all my food at once until I somehow come across more. Inside the bag there doesn't seem to be as much food as I thought, only two cans of Spaghetti-Os, an apple, and a few sleeves of Saltines. There's hardly even enough food for me to waste my time rationing. This isn't going to get me far at all, and I'm going to need to figure out something soon. Regardless, I reach in for the apple.

Reading the rolled-up chart is going to be easier to do if I spread it out on a large, smooth rock, rather than in the sideways mess of the little cabin. Grabbing both the chart and apple, I step out through the companionway hatch. Unfortunately, my left foot catches on something, slamming my chest hard into the cockpit seat. OOFFF! All the air's knocked out of my lungs, and the apple flies out of my hands and over the side. "Damn! That really hurt." Curling my knees to my chest I gasp for a breath, trying to get air back into my lungs. There are seagulls on the beach carefully watching me, and probably hoping I'll spill more food along with the apple.

Where *did* that apple go? Glancing over what's now the side of the sailboat, there's no apple, only a little splotch in the sand where it had hit, and a trail leading under the boat. Being a little more careful, and still trying to get my breathing back under control,

I slowly step off the side and onto the damp, hard-packed sand. On one knee, I bend down to peek under the boat and there's the damn apple . . . about three feet in. It appears to be wedged tight between the hull and the sand.

There's no food to spare; I need that apple.

I can probably knock it out with a stick, but I might be able reach it. I try that first. I take my shirt off so it doesn't get wet on the moist sand, and go flat on my stomach, reaching in as far as I can. My fingertips just touch it, so I shove my hand in a little deeper between a rock under the sand and the hull. Maybe I can get it to roll out a little further so I can grab it. I flick it, poke it, and claw at it, but the apple is just far enough out of reach that I'm not going to get it this way; I'm going to need a stick, after all.

But when I try to pull my hand out, something jams it tight. Holy crap! My hand's wedged snug between a jagged rock and the heavy hull of the boat. The rock must be big and buried just under the sand.

Don't panic, I tell myself. But I'm below the tide level. Here in Maine the tide will rise thirteen feet. If I don't get out, I'll drown in about six hours.

This is bad, really bad. I tug hard again, but that only makes it worse. I take a deep breath. "Don't panic, don't panic, don't panic," I say, over and over. I need to keep cool to think this through. I'm stuck, and it's going to be a slow, cold death if I can't get my hand free. The seagulls watching me are no help.

Before I realize it, an hour has already elapsed and I'm still stuck. Nothing has changed. I've tried everything I can think of to free my hand. I've even put my shoulder into the hull, attempting to rock it, but the wooden planks of the boat, which make it a solid seaworthy vessel, also make it quite heavy. It didn't budge an inch. Now I lie here with the side of my face in the wet sand and my eyes squeezed tight. I want to cry.

Being stuck, time seems to speed up. The ocean has already begun its journey back up the beach, and, with every lap of wave, the water gets closer to me.

If I drown under this boat no one will ever know what happened. Maybe someone will find the boat drifting around or, more likely, washed up on the rocks. But who knows what'll happen to my body? Because no one's going to find it. I sure don't like the thought of this.

I am only thirteen; I'm not ready to die, and not ready to die is the whole reason I'm in this predicament in the first place. The police chief and mayor were trying to catch me, but if they did, at least they'd have finished me off faster than the tide will. I tug even harder at my now very sore hand. Still stuck.

There's nothing I can do about it. There's nothing anyone can do about it. There's not another person around for ten or twenty miles who can help.

But here I am, waiting to die.

How did things get so messed up, that I'm stuck in this situation? Was it all because of a dumb kiss? Probably not.

∞ ∞ ∞

Hours have passed and the seawater's already reaching the other side of the boat. That was fast! I swear it's coming in faster than I've ever known. It sure doesn't seem like it's taking six hours; it feels more like six minutes.

I scream, "Help, help, somebody help me!" There is no sound other than seawater starting to lap against the hull. I begin to sob; I wish my dad were here.

I miss my family more than I could ever imagine. It feels like there's some deep dark hole in my gut filled with a pain I've never known before. I even miss my sister. If she were here on the beach and saw me stuck under the boat she'd probably grin. She would really enjoy this as long as my dad was right here to free me. Even though she'd never admit it, I know she really wouldn't want to see anything happen to me.

And if my mom were here, she would probably have a nice peanut butter and jelly sandwich for me to eat while my dad worked to get me out from under the boat. I wish there was some way I could say goodbye to them.

Sand sticks to my face. The wetness of the sand soaks through my jeans. I can feel my body begin to shiver a little. I'm cold. I've never felt so alone before.

My heart stops. Is that what I think it is? Yes, it is. Water creeping over my hand! I'm still no closer to being free than I was hours ago. This is it the time has come. Oddly enough, I'm not scared anymore. Just sad. I just want to get whatever is going to happen over with. I'm so tired of waiting.

It seems as if my wish comes true. Now the water's past my elbow on my outstretched arm, and is quickly rising toward my shoulder. Time is accelerating even faster. Soon the tide reaches my chin, and if I dip my head down a little I can taste the salty water. The tide keeps rising as it has for billions of years; it doesn't care that I'm trapped under a sailboat.

The water is now to the point where I have to stretch my head to just keep breathing. But I know that, soon, even doing that isn't going to help. My hand and arm are numb, but I think I feel something different on my hand.

I'm too busy trying to keep my head above water to notice, but now I'm certain . . . the boat is starting to shift. It's going to start floating. But when? Hopefully sooner rather than later because I can't stretch my head any farther.

I force my shoulder into the side of the hull to try and rock it, but it's still solid. Nothing. The boat shifts a little more and there's less pressure on my hand, but I'm still stuck. I'm not going to be able to keep my head above water any longer.

I take a big, deep breath of air and duck under, tugging and wiggling the whole time when, suddenly, as it twists in the sand, the transom shifts and raises slightly. That's all I need! My hand pops free, and as fast as I can, I roll out from under the boat. The second my head's clear of the water I gasp, filling my lungs with air.

I'm free! I'm not going to drown on some lonely island by myself!

I run up to the dry part of the beach and plop down in the soft sand. The bright sunlight starts to warm my damp body and I notice the seagulls screeching and fighting over a crab. There's a sparkle to the water, a sign that the air's starting to move, and it seems to be out of a favorable direction. I can sail away from here! What a fantastic day to be alive. I shoot a fist into the air, "Wahooo!

« CHAPTER 10 »

Home

The sun on my body feels good while I sit on the beach as I continue to watch the rising tide slowly float the rest of the boat. It's still going to be a while before the keel loosens itself from the sand, but I have nowhere to go, and the trees and vegetation are too thick to do any exploring. I just sit and enjoy being alive.

I realize this is the first time I've gotten a really good look at the "borrowed" sailboat. When I sailed away it was pitch dark.

The boat has a traditional sort of look. The sides are painted a bright, snappy white with a red boot stripe at the waterline. The bottom of the boat, which at this point I know all too well, is painted with a heavy anti-fouling blue. Most boats these days are built of fiberglass, but this one has wooden planks that take a little more care and skill to build. Above the deck, only about a foot and a half tall, is a small doghouse that has two bronze portholes. The trim and other parts that aren't painted are varnished with such skill, they look like they're still wet. As the proud, yet temporary, owner, I'd say a picked a good-looking boat to make off with.

Then it hits me: What's the name of the boat? I don't know, and every sailboat has a name with, hopefully, a personality that fits.

I take the opportunity to walk around to the transom and see the name painted in black, with gold trim around each letter, *The Sticky Wicket*. I'm not too sure I know what that means, but, somehow, it seems fitting.

∞ ∞ ∞

Finally, *The Sticky Wicket* begins to float on its own, free from the sandy bottom that only hours ago almost killed me. I take my jeans off again and wade to the waiting sailboat, heave them aboard, and pull myself up through the lifelines. My feet are back on the deck and, for the first time, I'm starting to feel good about things. Time to get out of here!

Before pulling up the anchor, I'm *finally* able to get the chart out on deck for a look. I unroll it and have a good study to try and figure out where I am. After all, that was what I was trying to do before I got stuck under the boat.

With the chart unrolled, it's about three feet long, and the edges are a little chewed up from years of storage under the chart table. It's hard to keep flat.

I trace as best I can where I think I've sailed in the dark and fog. It shows a clump of islands that I'm pretty sure I'm on now, but I need to be certain. It's really important so I can have a confident starting point on the chart rather than just a good guess. The chart is a little confusing at first, but after I study it a little harder I think I know where I am. But it's still a while until I'm absolutely positive.

Studying the island I'm on now, it's clear it isn't much bigger than what I can see from here, so it's a good thing I didn't waste my time trying to explore it. However . . . if I was off exploring, maybe I wouldn't have gotten my hand stuck under the boat in the first place.

The chart shows great details from the depth of water to how many times a particular fog horn will sound to buildings on a particular island. I need to find an island where I can hide out, but even this detailed chart isn't going to tell me which one is best.

I notice one particular island just a little further to the east, much larger than where I am, with a small cove. It might have some potential. It's also only about six miles straight south of a mainland town, should I need to go in for any reason. I make my decision: that's where I'm going. It'll be my next destination, and according to the name printed on the chart, I'm sailing to Hunter's Island.

Now that I have a compass heading it shouldn't be too hard to find Hunter's Island even on a completely foggy day. But today is crystal clear, and once out on the open water, with a little luck, I should be able to see my destination. It's the perfect sailing day.

*** I'm up on the bow, ready to pull up the anchor, and the sails are already set, flapping in the light breeze and waiting to be trimmed in hard. But when I give a tug on the anchor rope, the boat hardly budges forward. I pull harder again, giving it everything I have, yet the boat only moves inches at a time toward the anchor. This is no good. I need to get that anchor off the bottom, but my thirteen-year-old body just doesn't have the strength.

I have to get out of here, but this island seems to be trying to keep me. First, by pinning my hand under the boat. Now I can't get the anchor off the bottom. What was that saying my dad always told me? "Brains, not brawn?" How in the world would brains get the anchor off the bottom? I sit on the bow, drumming my fingers on the deck.

It's funny how ideas sometimes come to me. Rather than a thought slowly forming like the simmering of a delicious stew, the good ones always seem to hit me over the head like a baseball bat. It's a good thing they don't hurt when they hit.

There're two winches in the cockpit used for trimming the jib and, sitting there, they might as well have said, "hey, dummy, raise the anchor with us." Without a second thought, that's exactly what I do: I run the anchor rope to the cockpit and around the winch, then start cranking on the handle as hard as I can. The boat begins to move forward until it's just floating above the anchor. I use the back of my hand to wipe the sweat off my forehead. The anchor gets heavier as I begin to pull its full weight up off the bottom. It may be slow going, but at least it's working. In another few minutes the sails are trimmed in and I'm sailing away from the little island that lured me in with the sandy beach for a landing.

∞ ∞ ∞

It doesn't seem to take long to reach Hunter's Island. Now that I'm only a half mile or so away, I'm starting to make out more details. On the north side of the island, protected from the sea's raging storms, there's a long dock with a second floating dock that rises and falls with the tide. Damn. I was hoping the island was abandoned, but a dock means someone may live here.

I fish out the binoculars from below to have a better look. It's hard to tell, things look pretty quiet and, as I get a little closer, there's no boat tied off to the dock. That doesn't mean anything, though; the boat that might dock there could just be out checking traps in the morning. To have a closer look, I sail straight for the dock. This could be the place where I'm going to stay for a while, a place where I'll be safe.

I just need a closer look.

I'm only a few feet from the dock and I can tell it hasn't been used in a long time. There's seagull poop everywhere, and old dock lines that the sun has all but destroyed. Looks like I'm the only visitor, except for the seagulls, that this old, wooden dock has seen in a while.

I give *The Sticky Wicket* a hard spin, as I've done many times aboard smaller boats back at the sailing club, pointing the bow straight into the wind and making a perfect landing. Yeah!

Once the boat's tied off, it's time to have a look around, so I head down the dock to check things out.. The island appears to be like the others I've passed; a rocky shoreline with a thick, pine forest. There's a path which leads up from the dock into the trees, and I notice a clearing further back in with a small building. All I can see is the roof and a single window but, whatever it is, it doesn't look too big. Halfway up the path are loosely stacked wooden lobster traps about the size of a large coffee table. They're very old. Each one's crusted with barnacles and covered with years of rotting leaves. I doubt they've been in the water in a long time.

Near the stack of traps is the small shack I saw from the water's edge. The door stands half open. The shack looks like it hasn't been used in a long time because pine needles have fallen through and weeds are consuming most of it. From what I can tell, it's likely abandoned.

Even though no one has used this place in a while, it seems to be in good shape. Maybe all it needs is a good cleaning.

A little uncertain of the situation, I step through the door to have a better look around. It's no bigger than my bedroom at home, but about the right size for a lobsterman to spend a few days off the mainland.

In the far corner, against bare, plywood walls, sits an old

army-style steel bed frame, rusting, and a mattress neatly rolled up in the center, as though someone plans to return soon. Opposite the bed is a small counter and a white porcelain sink stained brown with rust. But there's no faucet for running water; just the sink. Above the sink are two cupboard doors with God-knows-what decaying in there. I'm afraid to open them; maybe later. In the center of the little room, built from sturdy pine, and with years of stains, is a solid wooden table. Cleaned up, it should be perfect for me . . . maybe even better than my hideout back in Trent Harbor. This could work. I'm feeling better about the situation I'm in.

For now, I think I'll call this place home.

« CHAPTER 11 »

Wuss

Although I've decided to make Hunter's Island my home, I still have a big problem—no food. My stomach growls loudly and that, along with a dull pain, reminds me how little I've eaten in the last two days. And there isn't much food left from Sara's stash. The last can of Ravioli-O's didn't stop my hunger in the least. Now there's just enough food left to barely get me through a day, maybe two, if I'm careful. What started as mere hunger is now becoming irritating.

I need to learn to catch lobsters. They should be a good food source. Heck, I've got all the traps I need, so all I have to do is set a few. My food troubles will be over. There's only one problem: I hate lobsters.

Everyone I know always goes on and on about how delicious they are dipped in a little butter and salt. Not me—I can hardly stand to look at them, much less eat one. To me, they seem like large, oversized red bugs with pincers, furry legs and antenna. And they eat anything that drops in front of them, including . . . ugh, I have to stop thinking about it or I'm going to hurl.

Off to the side of the dock, where I came ashore, I notice there's an old dory, flipped upside down, hidden in the tall grass. I didn't see it at first because the bottom paint had flaked off with the seasons, leaving it a brownish color, like sand. I try to lift it but it doesn't budge an inch. With a lot of effort I'm able to rock it back and forth until I can flip it right-side-up. The little boat's a lot heavier than I thought. To my surprise, there're still two perfectly good oars tucked under the seats. This dory will work perfectly for setting lobster traps. I have everything I'm going to need except bait.

I have no idea what to use for bait. Even though I've spent my whole life in Trent Harbor, where most everyone in some way works with lobsters, I don't know what they use to catch the darn things. Thinking about it for a while, I realize it really doesn't matter; either way, I've got absolutely nothing to use.

I'm still thinking hard, the tide has long gone out and, still, no bait has magically appeared before me. The hunger in my stomach is beyond painful, and now I'm a little dizzy. Two seagulls are fighting over a small crab, each one trying to peck the crab before the other gull attacks. It's kind of entertaining to see which gull is going to win. Without a conscious thought, I pick up a good-sized rock and fling it at the two birds, sending them reluctantly away to safety. I walk over to the live crab. Its legs are still wiggling straight up in the air, and I'm thinking—people pay good money in restaurants to eat that? They sure don't look like this in restaurants. Cooked crabs right out of the steamer are pink and orange, but this one is sort of a brownish green from crawling through the muck.

With my jackknife in hand, the longest blade out, I give the small crab a good stab until it stops moving. His pincers look like they'll hurt if they get hold of my hand, so I wait an extra minute or two to make sure it's dead before picking it up.

Food, perhaps? Don't think about it too long, I tell myself, and crack off a leg. Putting the open end to my lips, I suck at the meat inside. Ughh! It's stringy, and salty, like a fresh-picked booger. My stomach twitches. Then it twitches again, only a little harder. Whooom! Out comes everything inside my stomach, which really isn't much.

Now what am I going to do? Eating raw crab is definitely out of the question. I'm missing home again, and begin to wonder what my mom might be cooking for dinner tonight. Sadness creeps over me in a way that feels suffocating. This whole situation just sucks. Why me? Why did I go home that way that night?

Back to the lobster idea. I look at the crab missing its one leg and wonder if a lobster would eat it. Probably not, but what else am I going to do? It might work as bait. With the knife still open, I crack and cut up the crab to get at the rest of the meat, and what little I'm able to remove, I pile on a flat rock. Because it's low tide, and the beach is exposed, I'm able to find two more crabs and do the same thing until I have enough to bait hopefully three traps.

All I have to do next is drag three traps down to the dory, load them up, row out a ways, and drop them in. Simple.

Back at the stack of traps, I grab hold of one at the top, tug at it, but it barely moves. Okay, I knew I wasn't the strongest kid around but I have no strength for this. It's frustrating; everything I need to do is hard—really hard. These stupid traps are going to kill me by the time I get them down to the dory; yet I don't give up, even though my dad thinks I'm just a lazy kid. I pull hard at the trap until it slides off the stack and hits the ground with a dull thud. That was one. I do that again with another two traps.

Dragging them down to the dory is no easy feat, either. It takes me awhile, and a real lobsterman would laugh at me. I just need to get three traps to the dory so I can bait them and load them up.

The next job's to get the dory into the water. Hopefully, it still floats. Grabbing hold of the transom, which has very little paint, and is showing bare wood, I try to pull it toward the water. Nothing. It doesn't move. I beat my fist hard on the hull several times, and then I kick it for good measure. The little boat refuses to move. "Why does this have to be so hard?" I yell in frustration. "I just need to eat."

I plop down in the grass next to the boat, with my face in my hands. I sit there for awhile, looking out at the sea, and think about the situation I've gotten myself into. It just doesn't seem fair. Why me? Here I am, all alone on this dumb island with nothing to eat, and I can't even get the stupid dory in the water! I'm just not strong enough to move it. But I refuse to give up. I can't give up or I'll starve to death. I have to keep trying.

It takes me about two hours to drag the dory across the beach and into the water. Afterwards, I'm so exhausted, I only load one trap. It sits on the seat in the transom. Soon, the sun is going to set. There's no time to feel sorry for myself, so I climb in, sit on the seat, and pull hard at the oars. The boat moves slowly through the water.

Away from the dock, finally, I wonder where a good place to set the trap might be. Again, I've no idea how this works. It seems to me, back home, whenever I look out on the water, the little colored buoys are everywhere, and most times right in the way of where I'm sailing. It's so annoying. Anywhere should do . . . I guess. So I row out only a little further, reasoning that, when the time comes to tend to them, I won't have to row too far. I might as well keep something about this operation easy.

I pick my spot. I make sure the coiled length of rope and buoy are secured to the trap. Grabbing the colored buoy and pulling up the rope's the only way to get the trap off the bottom. If the rope comes undone, I'll lose the trap and it'll sit on the bottom forever. I give it a shove into the water, the trap splashes, and I toss the coil of rope along with the buoy in after it.

The trap bobs in the water for a bit with the buoy to the side. The trap slowly starts to sink on its journey to the bottom but, without warning, the buoy also disappears under the water. What? It's not supposed to do that! It's supposed to float on the surface. I wait for it to pop back up, but it never reappears.

As I stare into the water in disbelief, I suddenly realize that this spot is way too deep, and the coil of rope isn't long enough. The trap has pulled the buoy down to the bottom with it. I am never going to see that trap again.

"Damn! Damn! Damn!" I shout at the top of my lungs, while I keep slapping the water with an oar. Too deep! It never even occurred to me. I just wasted all that time dragging the traps and dory down to the beach and caught a few stupid, slimy crabs for bait—all for nothing. And I don't even like lobster!

Frustration overwhelms me, and I just sit there on the wooden seat for a long time staring blankly at the sea. The water has a dark, cold personality, and it just devoured my trap. I want to cry, but I don't. Maybe I'm getting older? Crying isn't going to help me, anyway. I drift a little longer, maybe even for a half hour, until it's almost completely dark, then pull on the oars to get myself back to the island.

With the dory secured to the dock, I climb aboard *The Sticky Wicket*, go below deck, and crawl into the bunk. The last thing I remember is kicking off my shoes and listening to them hit the floorboards. Tomorrow is another day.

111

∞ ∞ ∞

When I wake in the morning, sunlight streaming through the bronze porthole, I notice that I've woken in the exact same position I fell asleep in. I can't remember the last time I was so tired. But today's a new day. I rub my eyes back to life as my dad's old saying keeps rolling over and over inside my head: "Brains not brawn, brains not brawn." Over the last few days his saying is starting to have more and more meaning. On this island, however, I need both brains *and* brawn.

I decide right here and now to stop feeling sorry for myself and get on with things. Yes, yesterday did suck, and things didn't go well for me. I was acting like a wuss. But, no more. Surviving on my own isn't going to be easy and, if I act like a little kid, I'm not going to make it. Bad things are going to happen. I just need to make the best of it. Today is a new start.

I still need something to eat, though. I take a moment to clear my head and think hard about what I'm going to do about it. *Use your brains*, I keep telling myself. And then, just like that, an idea strikes me. I take out my jackknife. Next, I carefully extract the heavy stitching from the cushion I slept on last night. I do it in such a way that it does no damage to the cushion; I'll just have to be more careful when I lay down on it. After that, I go up top to the rigging that holds the mast in place and remove a cotter pin from one of the turnbuckles. It's not easy, but I'm able to bend the cotter pin into a hook, which I then very carefully tie to the cushion thread. Even if it takes me a little longer, I want to be certain I'm not going to lose anything else to the bottom of the sea. Next, I comb the beach for crabs. Soon there's fresh crab meat on my cotter pin hook. Thanks, Dad. Brains, not brawn. I am ready to fish.

Not long after throwing my hook and bait in the water, I'm already finishing a meal of raw bluefish. I'm not too sure how safe it is to eat fish raw, but I remember reading in Social Studies the Japanese eat their fish this way. I think it was called sushi. Hmm….Social Studies actually helped me with something.

It took a few tries to hook a fish with a used cotter pin but, in the end, it worked. Now there's nothing left but a fish carcass. The meal filled the void, somewhat, but it isn't going to be a favorite anytime soon. It's only a little better than the raw crab, but at least I can keep it down. But, as hungry as I was, I can deal with it. The only thing I can do to improve the situation's maybe figure a way to build a cooking fire. Things are looking up. I feel satisfied with what I've done.

Now that I've food in my belly, I can think through the rest of my plan; the "brawn" part. I know Dad's saying really means to do a task easier, think things through, but if I'm going to live on Hunter's Island I also need to be stronger to survive. I need brawn.

Back on board *The Sticky Wicket*, notepad in hand, I begin to write out an exercise routine that'll hopefully make me stronger. I need to make some weights to start getting my arms in shape. There're plenty of rocks I can use for that. Running would probably help, too, but on this island there's little open space to run; there're plenty of other things I can do, instead.

I work up a daily schedule: First thing in the morning is a workout, which will be followed by some cleaning inside the shack, and any other chores that might need to be done to live on this island. Afternoons will be for fishing. It'll be a full day, but I have nowhere to go and I certainly have the time.

My time on Hunter's Island didn't start out well. Everything seemed to go wrong. But now that I'm able to catch something to eat and I have a plan in place, I think living on this island isn't going to be too bad. I feel good.

« CHAPTER 12 »

Cool, Man

Summer marches along; warm, sunny days filled with a daily
routine that keeps me busy. Several weeks may have passed, yet I'm
not too sure because I forgot to start keeping track of my days, but
I've kept to my plan; fixing up the shack and working out. It's
difficult to tell if I'm getting any stronger because it's such a gradual
thing, but I think a lot of the tasks on the island are becoming a
little easier. Like the other day, I needed to move some of the traps
around because they were in the way. I grabbed one and lugged it
around. No problem. All in all, though, it's a lot harder living here
on Hunter's Island than I ever could've imagined. But, boy does the
time go by!

 After cleaning out and fixing up the shack, I'm now living in
it instead of sleeping in the little cabin of *The Sticky Wicket*. Now
that it's cleaned up, it's not a bad place to live; I just wish it had
electricity, and oh what I would give for running water. Without
those two luxuries, it's a lot like staying in the cabins at the boys'
camp I go to most summers. But, unlike at camp, I'm the one who's
doing the cleaning, fixing, and everything else. I'm in charge! And
that feels good! I might be starting to enjoy all the hard work.

Most days I usually spend an hour or two lifting rocks as part of my workout. I need to put some muscle on my scrawny body. When I've gone through my rock-lift routine, if it's low tide, I go underneath the dock, grab hold of one of the planks, and do a series of pull-ups. I hate pull-ups. It's hard to say if the way I'm doing them has any effect on my muscles but, I figure, how can it not? At first it was all very hard but, lately, I'm getting used to it, and enjoy going to bed tired after a full day.

This morning, as I lie in bed waiting for the sun to come up, I make a mental list of what I want to get done today. In the darkness I stare at the ceiling, the wool blanket from the sailboat pulled up over me. Maybe I need to come up with a few more fishing lines? It would be great if I could catch more fish in less time. If nothing else, I sure could use a spare line. I don't want to go hungry if I lose one. So that's my big goal for the day; more fishing lines and hooks.

Eventually the morning darkness turns to gray, but I stay in bed a little longer until the sunlight actually creeps up over the horizon. I have things to do, but it makes no sense for me to fumble around in the dark or, at least, that's my excuse for lying in bed just a little longer.

When I roll out of bed I pull my pants on, drag my shirt over my head, find my shoes, and then head out the door to start my day. Strolling toward the dock there's something different. At first it doesn't register, maybe it's the dim light of early morning, but when I take a second look, it's quite obvious. Tied to the dock next to *The Sticky Wicket* is another boat.

My heart skips a beat. I stop where I am and look down toward the dock. The boat's an older wreck of a lobster boat, with big brown stains on the side, and faded paint that I think was once white. The name on the transom, in peeling black paint, reads *Catch of the Day*. The engine's exhaust pipe, which emerges from the cabin structure in the center of the boat, looks so rusted out that I can't figure out what's holding it together. Each window's so grimy that I've no idea how anyone can see where they're going. If it weren't tied to the dock, I'd say the boat was abandoned.

So the question is: Who docked it there? I'm certain there's no one else walking around my island, but someone has to be around. It's probably the owner of the shack. If it is, he'll for sure boot me out of here. All that hard work right out the window.

Cautiously, I make my way down to the dock. The morning's very quiet, with few noises other than a gull or two, calling out. Even the sea's silent, no waves and no sounds. Each footstep I make on the old wooden planks of the dock sounds like falling timbers in the quiet of the morning. I'm aware of my breathing, and can hear my heart pounding in my head.

I try to call out, "Hello?" but it comes out as a whisper.

I walk slowly closer to the docked lobster boat. "Hello?" I

say again, but a little louder this time.

Once I'm at the rail of the boat, I stand motionless and listen. Nothing. I lean over the side of the boat into the cockpit. "Hello," I say, louder, and more confident. Still nothing.

Quietly swinging my legs over into the cockpit of the boat, I feel like I'm breaking into someone's home. I peek into the cabin. There're a few rusted tools lying about, a heap of foul weather clothing that look like a rotting compost pile, and old food wrappers with empty tin cans. Sitting on the floorboard is half a bottle of rum that looks out of place because it's a clean, clear item among piles of junk and debris.

I hear a grunting sound somewhere forward in the cabin. Following the sound, I find two dirty socks sticking out of the forward bunk. The socks are attached to the feet of a man who's lying in such a way that he's either dead, or dead-drunk passed out. The smell of rum and bad breath overtakes me, making me gag slightly, which assures me that he's probably passed out.

Should I poke him awake? Or just let him be? Judging from the smell of rum coming off him there's no amount of poking that's going to wake him. What the hell, I think; I'll give it a try, anyway. There's an old oar that is split down the middle and missing half the blade. I pick it up and give the guy a shove. Nothing. I do it again, only a little harder this time. An arm comes out and swats like there's a mosquito, and then he's motionless again. One more time; I give the guy a couple of quick jabs.

Two bloodshot red eyes crack open and blink as the man tries, without success, to raise his head. Then a puzzled look comes across his weary face and he says, "Are you a little wood elf who's come for me?"

I think he's serious. I know I'm scrawny and small for my age, but I'm working out hard and I'm sure I'm growing, too.

"No," I say, a little irritated, then give him another shove with the paddle. "Who are you and what're you doing here?"

"Hey! That's so bogus. Stop poking me with that paddle." The smell from his rum drenched breath suddenly hits me like a fish carcass rotting in the sun and I have to try hard not to hurl.

"Wood-elf dudes don't attack people with paddles; at least I don't think they do," he says, through a slurry voice. "Man, I want to speak to the head elf!" And his head flops back down and his eyes close. He's out again.

There's not much I'm going to be able to find out from this guy, at least not right now, so the only thing to do is let him be. Before I leave, I pick up what's left of the rum and dump it into the bilge.

I go about my morning routine, as there's always plenty for me to do, but keep a constant eye on the lobster boat for any sign of life. I wonder if I ought to get in *The Sticky Wicket* and get the heck out of here while I can. He could be trouble. The other half of me reasons this guy's probably harmless, so I might as well stay put, seeing as I've already put in a lot of work making the place livable.

A little before noon, I see the guy slowly climb out of his boat onto the dock, and look around like he's landed on Mars with no idea how he got there.

I watch him from up in the woods on the hillside, where I know he can't see me. The guy is skinny—really skinny. His stained and grimy jeans hang loosely on him, and his tightened belt is doing all the work holding them in place. His plaid flannel shirt long ago lost its sleeves, and his bare arms are deeply tan, with some sort of tattoo that I can't make out. He wears a well-worn, trucker's cap on his head, with a pony tail sticking out the back, and his beard looks like it hasn't been trimmed in years. He might be twenty years old or maybe even thirty, but it's too hard to tell because he is so shaggy.

Eventually he stops swaying, turns, and then stumbles off the dock onto the path that will lead him up to the shack. *My* shack. I'm not too excited to have him see that I've taken it over because he may never leave, but short of hitting him over the head with a rock, there isn't much I can do. I just stay out of sight and keep an eye on him.

After watching the confused guy trying to figure out where he is, I eventually call out, "Hey! You!"

He turns to see who said that, and I step out from behind a pine tree. "You there!" I attempt to talk in a much deeper voice, which really only sounds like a little girl who's trying to imitate a man's voice. "What are you doing on this private island?"

His eyes squint as he looks me up and down, and he picks at his beard. "You here alone?" he asks.

Thinking quickly, I say, "No, my dad's out fishing. He'll be back soon."

"Oh," the man says. He seems to be deep in thought, weighing my words. "That's cool, man." Still rubbing his beard, he says, "Am I starved. Got anything to eat?"

"Just bluefish."

I don't think that interests him. He then says, "Well, how about a cup of coffee? Your mom must have some coffee going."

"Nope, just bluefish. That's all I . . . *we*, have. Just bluefish."

"Just bluefish," he repeats. "I can dig it. Bluefish will have to do."

He shoves a hand out, and when he smiles he reveals a gold-capped front tooth. "Hey man, my name's Pete. Everyone calls me Skinny Pete."

It can't hurt to feed the guy. As long as I keep up the illusion that my dad's out fishing, and will be back, Skinny Pete will probably want to leave before too long. I lead the way up to the shack.

When Pete first steps inside, he squints for a while to let his eyes adjust to the darkness. Once they have, he takes a good look around. His eyes stop on the single bed in the corner, the only bed in the little room, but he doesn't say anything and sits down in the only chair at the table.

I hand him a plate of fish left over from this morning, but he doesn't start eating it and only pokes at it with his fork. Skinny Pete looks up from the plate with a disappointed look on his face. "It's raw," he says. "You eat your fish raw? That's harsh, man."

Suddenly, he bolts upright and dashes through the door. A second later he makes a cry that sounds like someone's turning his guts inside out. The thought of raw fish must not have agreed with him. About a minute later, Skinny Pete marches through the door and sits back down at the plate of raw bluefish, and slowly he begins to poke at it with his fork, taking a few timid bites.

"Why don't you cook your food on that stove over there?" he asks between mouthfuls, pointing to the wood-burning stove in the corner.

Because that would require me to chop and split firewood and would take me an awfully long time each day. It's all I can do to keep up with the things I need to do throughout the day, and if all I have to do is eat my fish raw to eliminate one hard chore, then I'm going to learn to eat it raw. But instead, I say, "We like to eat bluefish raw."

Skinny Pete looks up from his plate and said with a questioning stare, "You like your fish raw?" I don't think he believes me.

Without saying anything else, he stands up from the table and slowly walks around the tiny room while carefully eyeing everything. At the single bed he stands over it for a moment, taps it with his foot, then moves on to the "kitchen," carefully looking at how things are arranged. He runs a single finger along the counter top, then turns around, leaning his body against it, with his arms crossed.

"You know what I think, Little Dude?" he says. "I think you live here alone. I don't think your old man's out fishing. That's cool, we're all hiding from something, I don't need to know what you're running from," he says with a smile that tells me he's running away from something, too. I remain silent.

"Don't worry; I won't turn you into The Man. I don't care what you're hiding from."

Still, I say nothing, and give him a look that says I don't really care what he thinks. He works a hand through his wild beard while his mind tries to rummage through all its rum-soaked parts.

Eventually he says, "I'll make you a deal, man. My lobster boat is a lot of work; more work than I want to do in a day. How's about you help me haul traps, then I'll run them to town. I've got a dude who buys them freaky little critters and pays me good ching. I'll give you a quarter of the dineros; I need some of the dough to pay for juice for my boat, and bait for the traps." Skinny Pete sticks out his hand to shake on the deal.

I have nothing to lose, and some cash might come in useful at some point, so why not? Besides, maybe I'll learn a thing or two if I can keep him sober enough to keep working. I take hold of his hand and give it a hard shake.

"Cool, man," he says with a grin, shining his gold-capped tooth. "Cool."

Then, as if a great scientific breakthrough has just entered his brain, he says, "You know, I think I have a couple of cans of beans down in my boat. If you get a fire going in the stove, I'll cook us up some grub."

Skinny Pete begins to walk out the door then, stopping halfway through, he quickly turns around. "Dude, I don't know your name."

"Fisher," I say, before I realize it might be wise to make up a fake name. "Fisher," I repeat.

"The Fish Man . . . cool." He smiles, then continues out the door down to his boat at the dock.

« CHAPTER 13 »
Ice Water

A week, maybe more, has passed and I've been working harder than I ever have before, lobstering on Skinny Pete's boat. I'm finally getting the hang of things. It wasn't easy at first. For the most part, I'm the bait guy. It's not glamorous, but it has to be done. With the old, squeaky winch that's mounted close to the helm, Skinny Pete hauls the trap out of the water, sets it on the rail, and reaches in, grabbing the lobster. If they're big enough, they're keepers, and get tossed in the bin. Next, I reach into the bait barrel for a handful of slippery bait, and reset the trap. We repeat this process all day long until it's time to head back. It's awfully hard work, and, by the end of the day, I'm usually wiped out. Most days, after the boat's tied up at the dock, I go straight to bed.

It's certainly harder work than I imagined, but I enjoy it—along with being out on the water. My favorite time is when the sun comes up and all the nearby islands slowly appear out of the darkness. And even though the bait is foul-smelling, with a stink that's nearly impossible to get off my hands, it isn't too bad. It's my job. I'm responsible for that part of the operation and, if I don't do it right, we aren't going to catch anything. It's dumb, but I'm proud that I'm doing a good job—even if it's just shoving a handful of rotten bait into the trap.

I wonder what my dad would think if he could see me working hard on a lobster boat. It's good work, not the kind of work that he would do, but it's something that people from Maine have been doing for generations. I think he'd be pleased but I'm not too sure. I know a few of my mom's and dad's good friends own lobster boats, so I don't think it's a job that he would frown on.

"Skinny Pete," I say, as the trap I just baited splashes into the water with the colored buoy trailing behind. "How much money do you think we've made?"

He's facing forward, looking out the smudged cabin window as he steers, then takes a quick glance back at the bin full of the big wiggling bugs people pay top-shelf prices for. "Oh . . . I don't know. I never really know until I have the cash in my hand. The price seems to change by the day, and it just makes no friggin sense to me. I show up with my lobsters and they give me some ching, man. I'm cool with that."

He works his hand through his beard as he aims the boat for the next pot. "I'll tell you one thing, man. I think we're doing pretty good. With your help we've been hitting more traps than I ever have, so I think it's almost time to run these little critters into town and turn them into some dinero." Then he adds, "Maybe tomorrow, I don't feel like it today." The next trap slides in beside the boat and we repeat the whole thing again. "Besides, the weather's starting to get a little rough, and I think we should be heading in soon."

He's probably right; the day started out sunny, but now is gradually turning gray, while the wind seems to be slowly building. We should try to be tied back up at the dock in the next few hours, where it's safe.

After a few more traps, Skinny Pete says from the helm, without looking back, "So how old are you? You seem pretty young to be out here on your own."

It's funny; because in all these days working together this is the first time he's asked me that. In fact, I don't even think he remembers my name. "I'm thirteen," I reply. He thinks about that as he works his hand through his beard and steers the boat to the next trap.

"Thirteen, huh? I remember thirteen," he says. "I had an awful crush on this girl in my homeroom, but I don't think she even knew I was there. I was always too afraid to talk to her. I should've talked to her, man." Skinny Pete doesn't say much after that; he's too busy staring at the horizon beyond the bow.

I open up the top of the next trap that Skinny Pete brings up but it's empty, so I refill it with fresh bait before pushing it back over the side. With a splash, it sinks out of sight.

Skinny Pete then says, "Do you have a girl like that; one you have a crush on? If you do, don't ever look back, and say, 'I should have.'" He smiles, but there's a kind of lost, faraway look on his face. Then he says, "In fact, don't ever look back on your life and say, 'I should have' to anything; you dig what I'm saying?" He continues to run his hand through his thick beard as if the answer to life is hiding somewhere deep inside it. I'm not sure I know what, exactly, he's talking about, but I think I have a vague idea.

"I sort of have a girlfriend," I say, as the next trap comes to the surface. But after I say that, I'm not too sure, because we've only kissed a few times . . . so does that make Sara my girlfriend? There really aren't any rules about that sort of thing and, honestly, I never paid any attention to the other kids in my class who were "going out." I wonder if Sara thinks of me as her boyfriend? Maybe she's just one of those girls who goes around kissing guys more as just a fun thing to do, and doesn't think of it as anything more? I bait another trap and push it back into the water.

"Well, man, you're a damn hard worker for just thirteen. I've worked with a lot of dudes who talked a big talk but did squat. I'd take you on anytime as a deck hand."

A grin breaks out across my face. No one's ever said that to me before; certainly not my dad. I look out across the water, thinking about what he said, while I wait for the next trap to surface.

Without warning, the diesel engine makes a loud screeching noise, wheezes like it's being strangled, and then goes silent. Skinny Pete slams a fist into the side of the cabin and shouts, "Mother of

God!" Then he pounds his fist a few more times for good measure. I'm afraid to ask, but I do anyway. "What just happened?"

"We just rolled over the goddamn rope to the trap. It's wrapped itself tight around our prop. The engine's seized!" Skinny Pete slams his fist into the side of the cabin again, then throws his hat to the floor.

I look over the transom, but all I can see is a piece of rope floating out from under us. With the bellowing of the diesel engine now quiet, I can hear more things around us; like how hard the wind's really blowing.

The whole time we've been out, the weather's gradually worsened, with overcast skies and an increase in wind. I don't think a storm's blowing in, but in the last hour the waves are bigger, making pulling traps really hard. It's probably the strong wind that pushed us back over one of the lobster traps, wrapping the trap's line tightly around our prop. Now we're dead in the water, drifting.

"What're we going to do about it?" I ask.

"I don't know, man. Someone has to swim under the boat and cut all the rope off the prop, and it ain't going to be easy." I look over the side again. The water is looking kind of dark, and waves are slapping the side of the hull. It doesn't seem like a good idea for anybody to be in the water, especially under a pitching boat.

"Can't we get on the radio and call someone for a tow back?"

That seems to anger Skinny Pete even more. "No," he says flatly. "We *are not* doing that."

"How come? That's why you have the radio on board; to call for help when you need it. Well, we need help."

He looks at me strangely,, and it scares me a bit as his eyes, like daggers, bear down on me. "No! We are not going to call for help, and don't ask me that again, you stupid little troll!" He turns his back and stares out at sea.

"Is there any other way?" I ask, knowing the answer is no. I'm hoping he has some sort of lobsterman trick to free up a prop, like a big knife attached to a long, hooked pole. He just shakes his head.

"Are you going to swim under the boat?" I ask. "Somebody has to."

"No way, man. No . . . friggen. . . way!"

"Well what're we going to do? We'll drift out to sea, and no one will ever find us," I say, with a quiver in my voice.

"I have no idea," Skinny Pete says, his face starting to look a little ashen. "But there's no friggin way I'm going under the boat. I'd rather drift forever than go under there." Then, as if by magic, a rum bottle appears in his hand, and he takes a hard draw. He ingests a gulp of air and then another long hit. It's almost half empty!

Our situation's going from bad to ugly. At the pace Skinny Pete's hitting the bottle, it's only going to be a matter of minutes before he's passed-out drunk, and being dead in the water, with the weather starting to build, there's no telling what might happen to us. There's no way around it; I'm going to have to swim under the boat to cut the prop free.

I start to pull off my jacket, but my hands are shaking so much it makes it hard to hang onto the zipper. "Do you have a knife?" I say to Skinny Pete.

A laugh begins to boil out of him as he sits himself down in the helm seat and the rum bottle clanks next to him. "You're going to jump over the side and cut us fhreeeh." Slurring his words, he laughs harder and takes another draw off the bottle.

In my pocket, I can feel the knife Sara gave me. I pull it out and flip open the largest blade to study it. It isn't the biggest knife in the world, but I keep it razor sharp; it'll do the job. Whenever I look at it, it reminds me of Sara, which is comforting. If I were to lose it in the water I'd be sick. With a length of line I tie one end to the knife and the other end to my wrist.

This is it; I'm going to do it. I drop my jeans to the deck and stand there in my underwear, goose bumps popping up, looking over the side into the darkening water. I close my eyes, and trying not to think about what I'm about to do, slowly count down from ten. ". . . three . . . two . . . one." And then I leap over the side, hitting the water feet first.

"HOLY MOTHER OF GOD!!!" I scream the second my

head pops up to the surface. The water's ice cold and I can hardly breathe. It's like someone hit me in the stomach with a baseball bat. Maine water is *cold*!

On instinct I start swimming *away* from the boat to build up some warmth. Then, after a few hard strokes, I turn around and swim as fast as I can back to the boat. The water's so cold it's painful. The split-second I'm at the side of the boat I grab hold of the rail and hoist myself back in, flopping on the deck like a hooked flounder. Scrambling back to my feet, I jump up and down by the rail, dripping cold, salty water, and look back down at the dark water.

I'm going to have to get back in, there's no other way, and by now Skinny Pete's probably too drunk to even stand up. I don't see him anywhere so he must've stumbled down to his bunk.

I try to calm myself so I can breathe normally and take deeper breaths to swim under the boat. It's going to be cold, I tell myself, so don't let it bother you. I'm just going to pretend the cold water's like those guys who walk across red hot coals . . . it's all in my head. I'm going to tell myself it's only a feeling; nothing else.

Without another thought, I leap over the side and let myself sink under the surface—then swim straight for the prop. Yes, it's damn cold, but I put it out of my head so I can focus on the task at hand: free the prop.

Though it's in front of my face, I can barely see the tail of the rope that binds the prop, so I grab hold of it to use it to pull myself closer to where I need to be.

Swimming under the wildly pitching boat's like trying to crawl under a bucking bronco. Growing on the bottom of *this* bronco, however, are sharp barnacles that'll cut me to shreds. Sure enough, seconds later, before I'm even near the prop, the lurching boat scrapes my forehead. Luckily it's so cold, I don't feel the wound to my forehead. It's numb. I remind myself to be extra careful and stay clear of the boat hull. My life depends on it!

Once at the prop, through the darkness, I can make out a mass of rope bundled tightly around the shaft. With my knife in hand, and the blade already out, I attack it, cutting ferociously. I don't want to be under the boat a second longer than I need to be. The rope's thick, and the few seconds of cutting doesn't seem to do a thing. But my lungs feel like they're going to explode, and I have to resurface.

I pop my head above the surface and suck in air as if I'd just sprinted a half mile. While treading water, the salt stings my eyes. I need to build up the courage to do it all over again.

Before I can chicken out, I dive under the water and attack it once again with my jackknife. It doesn't get any easier, and the progress is almost zero. Am I even cutting through the rope? I wonder. I need to get this done fast because in this frigid water my strength and energy's almost done! Five more minutes in the Maine water and I'm just going to be a floating, blue corpse. I resurface a second time to regain my strength.

Before hypothermia can set in, I dive down again, knife in hand. The whole process of trying to cut through the thick, bound rope is beginning to seem useless, but I keep at it, pushing the knife as hard as I can. The pain in my lungs is beginning to feel like fire. I want nothing more than a deep breath of fresh air. The urge to suck in is unbearable, but it would be cold sea water filling my lungs, drowning me in seconds. I've always heard that drowning's not as painful as one would think, but I sure don't want to find out for myself. I cut even faster. Suddenly, the knife hits the bronze of the propeller shaft; I'm through. With my other hand I grab hold of the rope and pull it all off as effortlessly as noodles falling off a fork. Without a second to spare, I shoot to the surface.

When my head breaks free I clutch the side of the boat and I take in big volumes of air. Oh . . . that feels good!

I'm exhausted like I just sprinted a mile—and won. I did it! I really did it! I throw my fist in the air triumphantly! But there's no one around to tell me I've done a good job. Who cares? I don't. I know what I've done.

The prop's freed up, the engine should start, and we'll be able to head back to Hunter's Island. Bobbing there in the water, I see that the sky has gotten a little darker, and that the wind has chopped up the sea more, giving it all a very sinister look. We need to go.

After my breathing slows a little, I'm able to climb back up over the side of the boat and collapse onto the deck.

Laying here on the bait-stained deck, I don't feel cold at the moment because the air, compared to the water, feels so much better. I remain here for a minute longer, watching the gray sky above.

There're some old rags piled in a corner that smell awful, but I use them anyway to dry myself off, and then I get back into my clothes. But now's when I really begin to feel a deep cold, and shivering overtakes my body.

Looking down below, I can see Skinny Pete's feet hanging off the end of the bunk. He's passed out; much like the day I found him that morning when his boat showed up. Again, just like that day, I go down below with a broom handle and give him a hard poke. Nothing. I really want to hit him over the head with the handle, but he's out cold and would never feel a thing. He'll probably remain this way until tomorrow morning.

I'm going to have to drive the boat back to the dock myself. It's no big deal because I've driven the sailing club's launch many times, so it should be a lot like that, only bigger.

I push hard on the starter button. The starter motor below the floor boards whines loudly as it turns the diesel engine over. Bang! A big puff of black smoke shoots out of the exhaust, but the engine's running. It's a little rough at first, but then it starts to settle down, thumping away into a nice, easy rhythm as diesel engines do. When the engine sounds like its running solid, I ease the shift lever forward and gently give it some throttle. The boat begins to glide forward through the water. Yeah, man! I did it! We're heading back, and it's no thanks to that drunk below. A smile spreads across my face that I can't contain.

« CHAPTER 14 »

Captured

The little shack's beginning to fill with light from the glow of the early morning sun streaming through the window. I flip the covers off the bed and stand up as I remember the events from yesterday.

It was pretty crazy to jump over the side of the lobster boat into water so cold it could've killed me. But it had to be done, or there was no telling where we might be right now. Anything could've happened. We could've drifted up against a rock and smashed the boat to pieces. I did what was needed and I'm proud of it. Someday I'm going to be able to tell my friends back in Trent Harbor all about it.

Ahh . . . Trent Harbor. I wonder what my friends are doing back home. Suddenly, once again, there is the pang of homesickness, which has become all too familiar over these last weeks. I'm not sure how much longer I can stay away, hiding on Hunter's Island. My mood goes from proud, to sad, and stops at lonely. I'm getting so tired of it.

Before I put on my shoes to head down to the dock, there's a little fish wrapped up, left over from yesterday, which I grab for my breakfast. Each day the fish seems to get tastier. I suppose when that's all you have to eat you learn to like it after a while. I sure wish I had some peanut butter and jelly.

Not surprisingly, there's still no sign of Skinny Pete down at the lobster boat. And when I look in, it's just like the day he arrived—he's still passed out in his bunk from the day before.

This time, I grab him by his shirt and shake him hard. "WAKE UP," I yell. "Get up, you stupid drunk."

"Whoa, man," he manages to say, as he struggles to open his eyes. "What's your deal? Why are you so harsh?" His head comes up, then flops back down on the bunk. "Be cool, man."

"What's the deal? What's the deal!?" I kick the bunk, hard. He looks at me with pure hatred, but he's too soaked with rum to do anything about it. "We could be washed up on a rock somewhere out there, and no one would find us. And you did nothing but drink." I give the bunk another kick and leave the boat.

I'm frustrated, and need to burn it off. The tide's out, so I go under the pier to do some pull-ups. It stinks under here, as it always does when the tide's out, but I don't pay attention because the pull-ups make me feel better. Without too much problem, I'm able to knock off a lot more reps than when I first started. Next, I do my rock lifts and rock curls. They, too, are becoming easier, so I push myself until I break out in a sweat. I must be getting stronger.

It's funny, but I don't feel as scrawny as I used to. I don't know if scrawny *is* a feeling, but as this summer goes by, I feel less like a runt. Lately, my clothes are feeling a little tight, which is soon going to become a problem. I'm not too sure what I'm going to do about that, but I'll figure something out.

"Dude." It's Pete, above me, on the pier.

I stop lifting the heavy rocks and say nothing for a moment. I'm not sure I want to talk to Skinny Pete.

"Dude," he calls out again.

I sigh. "What do you want?" I yell up to him.

"I think it's time we take all these bugs we've caught and sell them for some dineros."

That gets my attention. It sounds like a great idea to me because lobsters make pretty good money. I scramble up the bank, and then onto the pier, where he's sitting with his legs over the side. I sit down next to him

"Where're you going to sell them?" I ask, in a low voice. I'm still mad at him for yesterday.

"Wyman Cove, man. It's about seven miles or so from here. There's a dude there I usually sell to who doesn't ask too many questions. Are you hip with that?"

That doesn't sound right to me. I say, "What do you care if anyone asks questions? What do you mean?"

He's staring at his feet hanging off the pier, "I don't mean anything. The man just takes what I have and gives me a fair price. No hassle."

I think about that, and say, "I'll help you load them up, but I think I'll stay behind. I've got things I need to do."

He looks right through me with his bloodshot eyes. He knows there's a good reason I don't want to be seen in any town. "All right, I'm cool with that. You help me load up, and I'll run them in. I'll use some of the dough for fuel, then we'll split the rest. Slap me some skin." He holds out a calloused hand for me slip him some skin as if that'll erase what happened yesterday. Maybe it does, maybe it doesn't; I let him hang.

∞ ∞ ∞

We spend most of the morning filling up tubs with fresh seawater on the back of the boat, then transferring our catch of lobsters from the past weeks into them. All available tubs are filled to the brim with salt water and lobsters. It's been a good couple of weeks, and for me, who's never earned money before, it's like looking at barrels of money. I'm excited. I may be hiding out, but at the same time, I'm earning some good money. Even better money, probably, than if I'd been busing tables at the Sea Side restaurant.

The diesel engine's been warming up for the last fifteen minutes, and every last lobster has been loaded on. I'm just about to cast off the lines when I say, "Skinny Pete. Do you think you could bring back some hamburgers? That would be so good." He smiles and nods in agreement.

I add, "And maybe some peanut butter, too. That would be swell." He gives me a salute.

I toss the last dock line on board and give the bow a shove off the dock with my foot. Skinny Pete gives the boat some throttle, and black smoke chugs from the exhaust stack while he pulls away. Once again, I'm alone.

Skinny Pete may be a drunk, but at least he's someone to talk to. I throw a rock into the water, causing a few seagulls to jump into the air.

It's a quiet afternoon—the ocean's flat, and there're no waves crashing onto nearby rocks. Even the gulls are silent; they just stand on the beach, looking out to sea. The quietness of Hunter's Island feels out of place.

I head down to *The Sticky Wicket* and decide that today will be a good day to clean her up and do some straightening down below. I kill a good portion of the afternoon doing routine upkeep because it's just good seamanship to take pride in one's vessel. Also, I intend to return the boat to the owners someday in better condition than I found it. I'm probably in deep trouble for taking the little sailboat and, quite honestly, the owner will probably never notice I took good care of it while I was its captain. But I don't care. I'm going to do my best to keep it as nice as I possibly can.

I start by pulling up all the floorboards down below, and

sponging out the bilge. From there, I move on to straightening up the cabin and using the liquid soap that was stowed below to cleaning just about every surface, whether it needs it or not. After I'm satisfied I've done all I can do, I go back up top to the deck and start scrubbing the teak and polishing the brass. When the last piece of brass is shining, the sun is just about to set. The boat sparkles just as it probably had on the day she left the boat builder's yard. I go to bed, tired and exhausted.

∞ ∞ ∞

Something causes me to wake suddenly. I try to sit up in the bed, but I can't move! My legs are stuck, and I my arms won't budge. Panic sweeps over me like a wet blanket, suffocating me.

"HELP!" It's all I can do to call out. I fight furiously at whatever is holding me back, and feel a sharp pain dig into my wrists and ankles. I'm tied up.

A flashlight clicks on at the table in the middle of the room, and sitting in the chair is Skinny Pete.

"Just chill, Fisher Shoemaker. If you fight it you're only going to hurt yourself, you dig? You may think I'm a worthless, no-good drunk, but the one thing this drunk's good at is tying knots. But believe me, man, the last thing I want to do is hurt you."

"What's going on?" I demand, as I struggle against the

ropes.

"Well, you see, Fisher Shoemaker, it's like this. What do you suppose I saw when I pulled into the dock at Wyman Cove?"

I shake my head; I have no idea.

"There were posters stapled to telephone poles with your name, Fisher Shoemaker, under a picture of you. And guess what? There's a $5,000 reward if anyone's seen you or knows of your whereabouts. I said 'Pete, that's a heck of a lot of moolah,' and guess what . . . I *have* seen you, and I *do* know your whereabouts. Cha-ching!" He starts whistling, "We're in the Money."

I'm in shock. I guess my parents didn't buy into my park service story. How could that not work? I suppose I knew all along it wasn't going to fly. Suddenly, I realize that, for them to offer reward money, and money they probably couldn't afford, they must've been really worried about me. I surely don't want them to worry about me.

"You *cannot* take me back. They'll kill me."

"Man, don't you think you're being a little dramatic? Your parents aren't going to kill you; they're probably worried sick about you."

"Not my parents," I say, with panic in my voice. "The guys who saw me watching them put a dead body into the trunk. They want to kill me!"

I'm not sure why, but I don't want to reveal that the guys

were the police chief and the mayor of Trent Harbor; it just seems like it might make it all the more unbelievable to someone like Skinny Pete.

Skinny Pete thinks about it for a moment while he takes a bite of a cold hamburger. With a mouthful of food, he says, "You were right; a hamburger *is* better than eating cold fish."

Then he stands up and picks a little piece of ground beef from his beard that had dropped from the sandwich. "You know what I think? I think you are a thirteen-year-old boy with an active imagination. Five grand's a lot of dough for a guy like me, so I'm still going to turn you in." He chuckles.

Clearly I need to take another approach because he doesn't believe I saw a body being loaded into a trunk.

"With me helping you, we should be able to make that much money catching lobsters. Probably more. Why would you want to give that up?"

He's silent while he finishes the last of the cold hamburger. He wipes his lips with the back of his flannel sleeve, then says, "There's a part of that plan that just won't work. You see, those traps that we've been working, well, they ain't really mine. We've been poaching."

Aw, crap, I think. Now I'm in trouble for poaching, too. In Maine, that's as bad as horse stealing. I'm pretty sure they won't hang us, but I do know the lobstermen, in their own way, will get us good!

There're always stories of the new guy who starts lobstering where he shouldn't, only to have his boat cut loose from the mooring, or worse . . . simply sunk. And this is FAR worse in their eyes than some newbie setting traps in the wrong place. If we get caught, we're screwed!

"Why would you do that? You couldn't just buy your own traps and set them? You had to steal lobsters out of other people's traps?"

"Too much work to do all that," he says. "I'd have to buy them, get a license, maintain them, pull 'em out of the water each year, find a place to store 'em in the winter, and then put 'em all back in the water in the spring. And nobody's going to let me just show up and start throwing traps into their territory; it don't work like that, man."

He starts to shine the flashlight around, as if he's looking for something. "Damn, there's no rum in here. How can anyone have a lobster shack without rum?" He steps out the door for a second, then steps back in.

"It's lucky for me I parked one just outside the door." Skinny Pete unscrews the top and takes a big gulp. I can almost see rum working through his body, then a satisfying smile grows across his face. "Man, that's SWEET."

"The way I see it," he continues, "it ain't too heavy. I ain't hurting anyone by taking a few of their lobsters. Hell, we're putting bait back in the traps so when they show up there might be a fresh new lobster lounging in there."

But, I think, *there might not be* any *lobsters.*

"No one knows—no one loses any ching," he says. "I take a few, sell them to the dude in Wyman Cove, and move on." He stops talking, and I can see his mood's quickly changing. Suddenly, he slams his fist to the pine table, causing it to jump.

"Hell! Why are we even talking about this? It's what I do, okay!" Skinny Pete takes several more big gulps from the bottle, draining a good portion of it. It doesn't take long before he starts wobbling, and needs to sit back down in the chair. As if it takes everything he has left, he snaps the bottle to his mouth and finishes off the remaining rum. His head careens side to side, as if it has just doubled in weight, then hits hard against the table. He's out; hands still clutching the empty bottle.

The room's now silent, but there's still light from the flashlight. I'm bound to the bed. But now that I'm not panicked I remember, once again, my dad's favorite saying: *brains, not brawn.* It's obvious that "brawn" has already hurt me because when I struggled the rope cut deep into my hands.

I realize that the way Skinny Pete has me tied down, it's actually only the mattress that's keeping things tight. If I can wiggle the mattress around, the rope might become loose enough to get out. Brains, not brawn.

The bed's not much bigger than a cot, so I start shifting my weight to rock the whole frame. Bump . . . bump . . . bump. The bed bumps from one set of legs to the other, the momentum building, the intervals between bumps growing longer and longer. With one big shift of my body, I manage to rock it hard enough so it hangs for what feels like forever balancing on two legs, then—WHAM! I crash hard to the ground, slamming my face into the solid pine floor.

OOOUFF! Man, that hurts! Lying on my side, I can't do anything until the pain goes away. While trying to get the air back into my lungs, I realize the mattress has shifted just enough so that the rope holding me is now sloppy. I wiggle my right hand, and almost effortlessly, it pops free of the rope. My other hand comes out just as easily, and in no time, I have my legs free as well. Skinny Pete's not as good at knot-tying as he boasted because here I am standing over HIM!

∞ ∞ ∞

Now that Hunter's Island has been my home for most of the summer, steering Skinny Pete's lobster boat out through the channel is almost second nature. The sun won't be up for maybe an hour, but I can easily find my way out in the gray morning light. I know the rocks, the shoals, and where the waves are breaking. It's no big

147

deal.

After I'm well clear of any islands or hazards, I bring the throttle back to idle and shift it into neutral. We drift, and the diesel engine putts away quietly in the background. I gaze back at Hunter's Island, which seems to be at least a mile away. It'll be a long row back but I can do it, no sweat. I've become stronger throughout the summer, so a little rowing's no hassle.

In fact, when I dragged Skinny Pete's passed-out butt from the shack down to his boat, it wasn't any harder than dragging a sack of potatoes. Not that I know what it's like to drag a sack of potatoes, but I guess it must be sort of the same. I can now pull lobster pots all day long without a struggle. I also guess I've grown quite a bit because the few clothes I have are starting to look ridiculous on me. I'm going to need to do something about that soon, or I'll have a real problem on my hands.

Skinny Pete's still passed out in his bunk. I suspect, from the amount of rum he drank, he'll be passed out for a long time to come. That's good. Because my plan depends on it.

In his top shirt pocket, I find a neat roll of cash from the lobsters he sold. I pull it out, unwind it, and begin to count the money. It comes to about $600. Not bad money for a week or two, of work. I peel off $300, shove it in my pocket, and then put the rest back in Pete's shirt pocket. It seems like a fair split to me.

Back at the helm, I pull out the rope I placed there before

148

we left. I make sure the steering wheel's straight, and then I lash it so it won't move. With a few, quick tugs on the wheel, I'm satisfied it isn't going to budge. It should hold a straight and true course.

Well, this is it, I think to myself. This is the day I say goodbye to a lousy drunk who wasn't much of a friend. I really could've used his help given my situation back at Trent Harbor, but rum always comes first in his life. So, once again, I have no one to rely on but myself.

I move to the transom where the dory's tied off. Uncleating it, I pull it alongside the lobster boat, climb in, and while I'm still standing in the dory, pull myself alongside the helm.

There's no turning back now. I reach over, push the throttle a bit, and then bump the gear shifter forward. The lobster boat lurches ahead and begins to chug out to sea while I'm left still standing in the dory.

Pete will be okay. Once he comes to, he'll be far away from Hunter's Island so I hope he'll get the message he isn't welcome back. Depending on how dead-drunk he is, there should be enough fuel left that he can find his way back to shore somewhere. And he has enough money to buy plenty of fuel and food, so I certainly don't feel any guilt about sending him on his way. I watch the lobster boat chug away for several minutes.

Both the oars are in the locks. With a solid grip on each, I turn the dory back toward Hunter's Island. I pull hard to get the dory moving, and then begin to set a steady and true pace back to my island. It'll take a while, but it's no big deal. I got rid of the drunkard, Skinny Pete.

« Chapter 15 »
Wyman Cove

Several days have passed since I sent Skinny Pete on his way. I've fallen into a pretty good work routine, all of which involves setting my own lobster traps, or at least using the ones that've been left behind on the island. Now I'm able to row three at a time, stacked in the transom of the dinghy. With nothing but my hands and back, I can set them and check them. They're set in shallower water this time. I don't want a repeat of the first time I tried to set a trap.

After only the second day of setting traps on my own, I have more than enough sitting on the ocean bottom. All I need to do now is let them soak for a few days. I now have time to do other things.

All the rowing back and forth, dropping traps in the water, has given me a lot of time to think. According to Skinny Pete, my parents have a reward out for anyone who knows where I am. So that means they're worried sick about me. I need to do something about this.

I figure, while I have to wait several days, at least, for the traps to fill with lobsters, I should sail into Wyman Cove, where Skinny Pete sold the lobsters, and mail some letters home to let

everyone know I'm all right. My plan is to send a letter to my
parents through Sara, who'll be told to drop the letter in a local
mailbox. This way there'll be no postmark on the envelope. If my
parents were to see a postmark from Wyman Cove, they'd probably
find me pretty soon.

The other thing I keep thinking about is the fact that I'm
not going to be able to hide out on this island forever; at some point
I'm going to have to go home. I need to come up with a plan. The
situation with the chief of police, the mayor, and the body in the
trunk are not going to just go away. I've actually been thinking hard
about it all summer, but I still have no idea what to do.

I do, however, have a back-up plan just in case something
goes wrong, but hope I'll never have to find out if it's any good or
not. The plan has to do with the third letter I'm planning to mail.

∞ ∞ ∞

After I have most of my chores done for the day, I stroll down to
The Sticky Wicket to write my letters. There's a small pad of paper
and some pencils at the nav table, which will serve the purpose just
fine.

I sit down at the table, pencil in hand, and begin to write.
Dear Sara . . . and that's as far as I get. It's been almost the entire
summer since that night I sailed off. Maybe she couldn't care less

about me, and is hanging out with some other boy. I stare at the paper, clutching the pencil for at least a half hour. I know almost nothing about girls, and the harder I think about her, the more confused I get.

Eventually, I give up and just tell her I'm fine, that I hope she's having a good summer, and I tell her to "stay cool." I'm ill when I read it back to myself. It sounds like I've just signed her yearbook in the phony way you do when you want to be nice to someone, but you know there's no chance you'll see that person until the next school year. I don't know what else to do. I end it with instructions on what to do about the other letter, to my parents. I hope she doesn't tell them where I am. I fold it and just look at it in my hands. I'll have to get some envelopes in town.

While I'm still below, I switch on the VHF radio so I can listen to the day's weather report. I need to figure out when a good day will be to sail into Wyman Cove. Without any kind of motor on the sailboat, I need to make sure I have the right conditions or, at least, conditions that aren't going to kill me.

I always start out on Channel 16 because I like to listen to some of the other boaters chat. Sometimes they talk about the weather. Other times it's about how many fish or lobsters they caught that day, and sometimes it's even about their wives or girlfriends. I always make sure, though, I never listen to the chit-chat for more than a minute before switching over to the weather channel because I don't want to drain the battery. I have no way of recharging the battery here on Hunter Island, so once it's dead, that's it—no more weather reports. I need to make certain I only use it when I need to.

Today, no one's talking on the VHF radio. It's a little disappointing because it always makes me feel like I'm not so alone when I hear other boaters talking. Not today, though. I switch over to the weather.

Tomorrow's weather report sounds good. Just a nice, steady breeze in the right direction, but not so much that it could make sailing right up to the dock challenging. That's it, then. I decide that tomorrow's the day I'll go into town.

∞ ∞ ∞

Just as yesterday's weather report promised, the breeze is good. Wyman Cove's now ahead, just off my starboard bow. I can see what looks like a little community floating dock at the end of a long pier, and given the direction I'm sailing, it seems to be almost the perfect location. It shouldn't be too tough to make a good landing.

At about fifty feet from the dock, I ease the mainsheet out a bit to slow my speed. Then, as I glide closer, I give the tiller a hard push, spinning the sailboat into the wind and bringing it to a perfect stop right at the dock. I grin with satisfaction.

A minute later, the boat's secure with a bow and a stern line holding it fast to the dock. With the sails dropped, I stand on deck and take a look around.

Wyman Cove looks like any other little town on the coast of Maine. There are a handful of assorted boats on moorings, and all the buildings and shacks along the shore are mostly weathered gray cedar shingles—the result of years of salty air. From what I can tell, there looks to be a small town center just up the road from the pier. I would guess the post office has to be there somewhere.

I make my way up the long ramp from the floating dock to the pier. Over by the crane there's a lobsterman offloading his catch, and he's wearing black rubber foul weather pants with a red flannel shirt beneath. On his head, he has a dirty green cap that looks like it's been worn for a decade.

I can feel his eyes on me as I walk past. I keep my head up, trying to convey with confidence that I'm one of them. He doesn't say anything, but I'm a stranger in his little town. That doesn't always go over well with lobstermen. I can tell he's not impressed by my confidence. But I just keep moving ahead and hope he doesn't cause me any trouble.

At the end of the pier I stop, frozen in my tracks. There, in front of me, is a black and white poster stapled to the telephone pole with my photo. *Missing* . . . it reads, and sure enough, just as Skinny Pete said, there IS a $5,000 reward. Quickly, I pull the hood of my sweatshirt up over my head to cover my face as best I can. I look at the photo staring back at me. My mom and dad must have used my sixth grade photo from last year. Hopefully, I've grown enough that I don't look much like that anymore. I glance around carefully to see if anyone's watching me. When I'm certain no one is looking, I rip the poster down.

When I make my way off the pier onto the street, the town's even smaller than it looked from the dock. Sure enough, there's the post office right in the middle of Main Street, and across the street is the general store . . . and that's about it.

When I enter the post office, there, next to all the FBI's wanted criminals, is my poster again. Damn! I try not to look at it, or bring attention to myself, because this time, if I rip it down, someone will surely take notice. I keep my head down and walk up to the counter.

The balding postmaster scrutinizes me, then asks, "Can I help you, young man?"

Without looking at him I say, "Three stamps, please, and three envelopes."

"That will be a dollar twenty five," he replies, looking at me with narrowed eyes. He knows. He must know I'm the one on the poster. How can he not know? Be calm, I tell myself. Be calm.

I reach into my pocket and pull out the money I've taken from Skinny Pete.

"That looks like a lot of money for a fellow your age," the postmaster says with a suspicious eye.

Damn! How could I be so stupid? What was I doing pulling out all that money in front of him? "Mmmmhh . . ." Having no good answer, I mumble, and put two dollars on the counter. The postmaster slides my change back with the stamps and envelopes. The whole time his eyes never leave me, and he doesn't say anything.

Stepping over to the table, I write the addresses on the envelopes, drop them in the mailbox, and get out of there as fast as I can.

The next thing I need to do while here in town is find some new clothes. The ones I'm wearing are starting to look a little funny on me. Hopefully, the general store has something.

When I walk into the store, there's an older woman behind the counter sticking price tags onto some cans of beans that are stacked in a small wooden crate. She squints at me over her wire-rimmed glasses. Her gray hair is cut short and plain. Thin, stick-like arms poke out of her old, worn, green sweater.

"Can I help you?" she says cautiously, as if I'm here to shoplift.

"I just need some shirts and a pair of jeans," I say, trying to sound as though I buy clothes for myself all the time. Actually, my mom's the one who always buys my clothes, and honestly I have no idea what size I am. I guess I'll just have to try a few things on.

"Where is your mom?" she asks, not even hearing what I said.

I say, "Oh, she has to work today, so she sent me here with some money to buy clothes." I hold my breath, hoping she believes me.

"Where does she work?" she asks, as she pushes the crate of canned beans off to the side. Damn! Nosy old lady. Why does she have to keep asking me so many questions?

I pretend not to hear her. "Do you have any shirts about my size?"

Now standing in front of the counter with her stick arms tightly crossed, she says, "I know everybody in this town, but I don't know you."

I still don't answer, and go over to an aisle where there's a pile of work shirts. I start looking through them. The gray flannel in a "Large" looks like it should fit, so I pick it up, and then a second one, too, in green. I tuck them under my arm.

"Young man, what is your name?" she says, in a tone that means business.

I have to think fast. "Jimmy," I say. "Jimmy Page." I'm fairly certain she doesn't have any Led Zeppelin albums.

"Well, Mister Page, I think you should come back here with your mom. I don't know what you're up to, but I smell funny business."

I walk past her to the shelf where the jeans are folded and stacked, and start digging through them. I sort of remember my mom saying I was a size 28, so I figure that's my best bet because Mrs. Funny Business is not going to be any help. Finding a pair, I hold them up to see if they're going to be long enough because the jeans I'm wearing now are way too short, and my ankles are showing. I look ridiculous.

"I think these'll do," I say to the old bat. "I'd like to buy these."

With her arms still folded tightly, she looks down her nose at me, then says, "Then you should send your mom in here to buy them for you." Then she adds, "My husband owns the gas station, but he is also the police chief for this town. If you don't leave right this minute I'm going to call him."

I'm screwed! Trying to buy some clothes has gone terribly wrong, and now everyone's going to know I was here. In a town this size, it isn't going to take them long to figure out I'm the one in the "Missing" poster. Then, before I know it, I'll be dragged back home to Trent Harbor where the mayor and police chief are both after me. I'm more than just screwed; I'll be dead by the end of the day.

Reaching into my pocket, I pull out the wad of cash, peel off a twenty-dollar bill, and try to hand it to her. I look at her. She says nothing.

She slowly unfolds her arms, raising an eyebrow at me, then

reaches for the phone and dials zero. "Hi, Millie," she says into the receiver. "Can you connect me to Ed? I think he's over at the gas station this morning." She waits while Millie, who must be the operator for this little town, connects to Ed, presumably the aforementioned husband-chief-of-police.

Without a second thought, I slap the twenty dollar bill on the counter, scoop up the two shirts and jeans, and bolt for the door. I'm quick and doubt very much she'll be able to catch me before I get to the door.

The front door's nothing more than a screen door on hinges, so I put my shoulder into it and burst through, never stopping for a second until I'm in the street.

"Come back here!" she screams in rage. She really has no right to come after me; it's not like I'm stealing, and the twenty should more than cover the cost of two shirts and a pair of jeans.

I take off running, but not toward *The Sticky Wicket*. I don't want her to know I sailed in because then they'd come looking for me out on Hunter's Island. But in a tiny town like this, there aren't too many places I can hide, so the second I know I'm out of her sight, I quickly duck into an old shed along the water that has no lock on it.

Oh, my God! The smell is so awful that I have to fight back the urge to toss up my breakfast. Of all the bad luck—I'm hidden in a bait shack. With the summer sun beating down, the bait in this shed is the vilest smell I've ever experienced. I think the pit of an outhouse actually smells fresher. But I have to stay hidden, no matter what, until I know I'm in the clear. I close my eyes and slowly count to ten, hoping that by the time I reach ten I'll be used to the stink.

Inside, there are some small window panes that are so badly covered with God-knows-what that there's no way to see anything that's happening outside the shack. Very carefully, I take the sleeve of my shirt and clean a small area so I can at least look out. There she is, the old biddy, standing in the street trying to figure out which direction I ran. She stands there for a minute more then, shaking her head, gives up and goes back to her general store. I hope her husband, Ed, the police chief, will find little interest and not bother to look for me. Besides, I haven't done anything wrong. I paid for everything and probably had change coming back to me.

To be safe, I give it an extra five minutes before I poke my head out the door to see if anyone's looking for me. Man, the fresh air smells good! I don't think I ever remember air smelling so good. Another minute more in there with that God-awful rotten fish smell and I'm pretty sure it would've caused me some sort of brain damage.

As far as I can tell I'm in the clear but, instead of walking down Main Street, I find a path down by the water's edge that should lead me back to the pier where *The Sticky Wicket* is tied up. I think I'm fairly safe and hope no one will see me. I doubt anyone will notice me, but I'm not so sure they can't smell me a mile away. I walk along the path carefully, trying hard to look just like any kid playing outside.

Once back at the pier, all is quiet. Even the lobsterman who was unloading his boat has gone, so I take the path up to the pier and then head down the wooden ramp to the floating dock. *The Sticky Wicket* is waiting for me.

At last I'm back on board my boat. Without wasting any time, I hoist the mainsail, then the jib, and untie the dock lines. This is followed by a hard shove. When I sheet in the main, the boat begins to swiftly sail away from the dock. Goodbye Wyman Cove, hope I never have to come here again!

∞ ∞ ∞

The wind's blowing in a good direction to sail almost a straight line back to Hunter's Island, and I'm making good time. That's great, because I want to get as far away from Wyman Cove as I can before anyone starts putting two and two together; that I'm the kid in the posters . . . Fisher Shoemaker.

My stomach groans loudly, and I suddenly realize that I'm very hungry. It sure would've been nice if I didn't have to leave town in such a hurry. It would've been nice to have bought some good food, and maybe even find a restaurant, or a grill, where I could've gotten a cheeseburger. Mmmm . . . my mouth's watering just thinking about a nice, juicy cheeseburger, and maybe some crispy fries on the side. I'd have put just a little ketchup on it and a lot of yellow mustard. If I couldn't find a cheeseburger it would've been really swell to at least buy a few chocolate bars. Instead, I have nothing but more fish waiting for me back on my island. And now that I smell like a rotten fish, I have no appetite to eat fish . . . maybe I'll never eat it again.

About four and a half hours later, the breeze is still fresh and pushes the sailboat along nicely. I lost sight of the mainland about an hour ago. The day's about as nice as it can be, sunny and warm or, at least, warm for Maine, and just the right amount of wind for a great sail. It's a terrific day to be out on the water—despite the fact that I have no cheeseburger or chocolate bars. Soon, Hunter's Island appears on the horizon. As I get closer, it looks like it's slowly growing out of the sea. After my almost-disastrous day in Wyman Cove, it's going to be good to be back at my island.

The wind's still in a good direction to sail right up to the dock. Once again, this is more than I could ever have asked for. Soon the sun will set, and it'll be dark. I'm thankful that I haven't had to tack back and forth to make my landing. I'm thankful to be home.

Once the boat's tied up, and the sails are dropped, I make sure everything else is secure and put away. Before heading up to the shack, I figure it'll be a good idea to have a listen to tomorrow's forecast so I can decide whether I'm going to check traps or not.

I flip the battery switch and turn on the VHF radio. As always, I flip to channel 16 to listen to some of the boaters' chit-chat before going to the weather. The radio crackles, then I hear a voice I think I recognize through the static. "Whiskey, Foxtrot, Tango, Tango, one, three, niner; this is *Catch of the Day* to the Coast Guard station Salem Beach."

I stand up quickly, banging my head hard on the low ceiling, which knocks me back down into the bench seat. Man that hurt, but I barely notice the pain . . . on the radio is Skinny Pete.

"*Catch of the Day*, this is Coast Guard station Salem Beach; over."

"I'd like to report a stolen boat and possibly a runaway child, over."

Part III

« Chapter 16 »

Men in Blue

"**Catch** *of the Day*, can you repeat that location, please? Over," comes the crackling voice through the VHF radio.

"Yeah, man, that'd be Hunter's Island, just south of the town of Wyman Cove by about eight nautical miles. Over," says Skinny Pete.

"Thank you, *Catch of the Day*. We'll send a patrol boat there at the first light of day. Over and out."

I grab the pad of paper lying on the nav table and hurl it across the little cabin where it hits the forward bulkhead. With my head between my knees, rocking back and forth, I say to no one, "How could you, Pete? How could you!?"

But I already know the answer; I know why he's doing this to me.

I need to get out of here, and I need to do it now.

I race out of the cabin and up onto the deck, which is now in darkness. While I was down below, the sun set and total darkness swallowed the whole island and the sea. It doesn't matter. I know where every line leads on this boat, and I can sail it with my eyes closed—which I guess would be almost the same thing.

In a panic, I quickly raise the mainsail. It's not until I'm raising the jib that I realize the sail's not flapping, clanking, or making any kind of sound. No breeze. The wind has shut off completely, and it's a perfectly still night. I let go of the jib halyard and the sail drops back down to the deck in a heap. I'm going nowhere.

Standing on the deck, I look out into the black wall of night. I realize that in my panic, had there been wind, I would've tried to sail away. In the dark it would've been suicide. It's one thing to sail out of Trent Harbor with a lifetime of local knowledge and lighted buoys, but to sail out of Hunter's Island I would've, without a doubt, crashed on the rocks. The lack of wind probably saved my life.

With nothing to do but wait until the first gray of dawn, I figure I should at least come up with some sort of plan. One thing about this journey, I've learned it's always helpful to have a plan in my back pocket.

The chart of the area waters is still rolled up and stowed in one of the cubbyholes, so I carefully spread it out on the nav table. Even though I've spent the whole summer on this island, I still don't know what lies just beyond. So, even though it isn't much of a plan, I figure it can't hurt to become familiar with the chart.

I find Salem Beach Coast Guard station, which is much

farther to the east. Using the dividers, I walk off the miles between Salem Beach and Hunter's Island. It looks to be about thirty miles. Depending on what kind of boat the Coast Guard sends out, it'll probably cruise at twelve or thirteen knots. I pick up the pad and pencil to do the math. It takes me a couple of tries because math isn't my strong subject. After I check, and recheck, I'm fairly certain it'll take them about two and a half hours to make the island. And that's if they cruise in a straight line.

Whoa; it turns out math actually *is* useful for something. I'm going to make sure I pay more attention in school.

Looking at the chart again, I decide the best plan is simply to sail in whatever direction's the fastest. And that all depends on the wind. I hope to God it blows anywhere *away* from Salem Beach.

Now that math seems useful, I decide to try some more. I figure the fastest the little sailboat can move is probably about five knots so, with a two-and-a-half-hour lead time, that should get me about fourteen miles away before they arrive at the island—if I can actually sail at five knots. I pump a fist into the air. It'll be pretty hard for them to figure out where I am if I'm fourteen miles in any direction. And they may spend hours searching for me on the island before they realize I've fled, so that'll give me even more of a head start.

But there are several downsides to consider. What if there's no wind, or the wind comes from the wrong direction? What if the

Coast Guard leaves the station before the light of dawn and arrives at Hunter's Island before I even have the sails up? My head begins to spin with all the possibilities that can go wrong or right.

I flip the VHF radio back on and dial in the weather channel. Knowing which way the wind is predicted to blow tomorrow, and how strong, will rule out a lot of the possibilities. The weatherman's reading off all the meteorological data for today, which, for me, is useless. I couldn't care less how much rain we've had this month. I wait patiently for the forecast and chew at the dry skin on my knuckles.

Slowly, the VHF begins to fade then goes silent. All the juice in the battery has finally drained. No power. Hopefully, this is not a sneak peek at how things are going to play out for me. Sitting in the silence and dark is almost painful.

With nothing else to do, I fumble along the dark path up to the shack to collect the few things I have. It doesn't take long at all, so I go back to the little sailboat and climb into the bunk.

As hard as I try, there'll be no sleep for me tonight. There are just too many things racing through my head.

∞ ∞ ∞

Last night was about the longest night I can remember. If I slept, I sure don't remember doing so. But now the darkness begins to give way to dawn. Gray shadows appear very slowly across the water as I sit in the cockpit. I've been waiting hours for a little daylight to give shape to my surroundings. It feels like I've been sitting here for a week, yet there's nothing I can do but keep waiting. There is, however, a little luck on my side because the wind began to fill in about a half hour ago, and even though I can't see it on the water, the breeze on my face feels like it might be a good direction for an escape.

Gray shadows lighten the horizon and, eventually, I can make out rocks in the water and the outline of a few distant islands. It's time to go! Raising the main and jib only takes me a moment. I untie the sailboat from the dock, sheet in the sails, and begin to glide silently away from the dock. There's a little part of me that's going to miss Hunter's Island. It was hard, but I've made it my home, and I did it all on my own. I'm confident that if I can make a home out of this place, I can do almost anything I set my mind to.

When the sun peeks over the horizon, the wind freshens to almost perfect conditions. The boat heels over nicely, humming along with spray coming off the bow. The sails are trim and the boat's leaving a solid wake behind her. My hair, which has now grown long over the summer, blows out of control. This is perfect; the conditions are exactly what I need. A smile stretches across my face.

I have no idea where I'm headed, but for the time being, as

long as it's away from Hunter's Island, I don't care. Once I'm certain the Coast Guard will never find me on the vast open ocean, only then will I take a look at the chart to decide where to go.

According to my watch, I've been sailing for almost an hour. That's great because every hour of fast sailing means I'll be about six miles farther away from Hunter's Island. On open water, six miles is a lot. I just might escape from the hands of the United States Coast Guard. Screw you, Skinny Pete.

Puffy clouds race across the clear sky as the sun climbs higher. There've been no other boats on the sea. At least, there are none around me. Out here, I'm all by myself. It's just vast blue sea in all directions with only the scattering of islands way to the north.

Much later, I'm still heading in the same direction and sailing just as fast. I look at my watch again and am startled by what I see. Did I see that right? I look again. It's been three and a half hours since I left my island. I did it. I escaped! I stand up in the cockpit of the heeled boat and shoot both arms into the air. I can hardly contain my excitement. "Take that Pete, you stupid drunk!" I shout. I let out a huge, "WA-HOO!"

It's time to take a look at the chart and figure out where I am and where I need to go. I lash the tiller and hop down below to the nav table, where the chart's still laid out.

Knowing the compass heading I'm sailing, I use a straight-edge to pencil in a line on the chart to indicate the direction I'm sailing in. Next, I guess at my speed, then use the dividers to walk off the miles along the line I just drew. I stare at the spot I just circled on the chart. I certainly don't want to go there. I'm only seven or eight miles offshore, and fast approaching Trent Harbor.

The best thing to do, given my speed and the wind direction, is to alter my course just a little more to the south and sail right on past. If I do that, I'll still be offshore enough so no one will see me as I go past. I double check everything on the chart. By changing the heading a little I should be safe.

Back in the cockpit, I unlash the tiller and begin to point the sailboat slightly more to the south, paying close attention to the compass. Satisfied I'm on the right course, I gaze out at the horizon to see if I can actually view any land near Trent Harbor. I'm in the clear. But, in the opposite direction, I notice something. On the horizon is a boat.

The boat seems to be approaching fast. My hand hurts from squeezing the tiller so tightly. Chances are good it's just another lobsterman heading toward his traps, but I can't take my eyes away from it. I run my hand through my long hair. I remember a pair of binoculars are stowed below the chart table so, grabbing them, I quickly take a look. Damn! There, against the stark white hull, is the unmistakable red stripe; it is without doubt the Coast Guard.

How could they possibly have found me? I must be at least twenty five miles away from Hunter's Island, and I could've sailed off in any direction, making it nearly impossible. I squint through the binoculars again; they're moving fast. Certainly much faster than the twelve knots I thought they'd be going. At that speed, it'll only be a matter of minutes before they'll be right on top of me. There's no place to hide out here on the open sea. And, with the big white sails against the blue of the ocean, I might as well have a giant red arrow pointing to me; here I am!

Sitting in the cockpit, I close my eyes and try to think. *Brains not brawn, brains not brawn* . . . but not a single idea comes to me. There's no place for me to run, and the sailboat's much too slow to try and get away. Maybe I can make up a great story that the Coast Guard will actually believe. Unlike some of the other kids in school, I'm not very good at making up stories on the spot.

Some kids can make the teachers believe almost anything. Once, Brian Farwell had pulled the fire alarm just before a big test that he hadn't studied for. It got him out of the test all right, but it also got him a seat right in front of the principal. He looked the principal right in the eye and told him that, yes, he had, in fact, pulled the alarm, but he thought it was the light switch to the boy's bathroom. It wasn't much of a story, but he told it in such a way that the principal believed him and simply asked him not to do it again. He got away with it.

I need to think up a story like that, but within minutes, the familiar white hull with the red stripe is almost on my transom. I know the boat well; it's the U.S. Coast Guard's 41-foot UTB; UTB stands for Utility Boat. This one has two Cummings diesel engines with a top speed of about 26 knots. That's why it caught up to me so quickly.

All of us kids at the sailing club know every Coast Guard vessel; I'm not sure why. I suppose it's like farm kids being able to identify different tractors they see in the fields. But knowing about their boat's not going to help me at all in this situation. I'm a sitting duck.

A few minutes later they're following in my wake.

Remembering some of my sailing class, I stand up and make a big circle with my arms; the international signal for O.K. They aren't buying it.

Through the cabin-top bullhorn, a no-nonsense, monotone voice booms, "Drop your sails and heave to." I don't realize it, yet; I'm biting my nails almost to the skin.

This time I try yelling to them, "No! I'm okay. Thanks for checking on me." There's no humor in the men in blue uniforms who scrutinize me from the UTB boat. At least they don't have the deck gun pointed at me.

"Drop your sails and heave to!" The voice booms again.

I kick the side of the cockpit. Nothing will get me out of this mess. I shake my head and lean over to uncleat the jib and mainsail. Both sails drop to the deck, and the boat slows. I'm caught.

I'm in so much trouble that I'm probably going end up in some juvenile jail. This is not how I'd planned things.

When the Coast Guard boat pulls up alongside, it seems huge compared to my little *Sticky Wicket.* "Come on aboard," one of the men yells to me.

I feel like someone's sitting on my lungs and I can hardly breathe. There isn't much left I can do, so I climb out of the cockpit and hoist myself up over the side of the big white vessel, where two men instantly grab me by the collar and pull me in. Before I can protest they put a huge, orange life jacket on me that makes me look like a pumpkin with arms and legs.

The guy who looks like the first officer stands before me, "Are you Fisher Shoemaker?" His deep voice sounds like a guy in charge.

I nod my head, yes.

His eyes are hidden behind a pair of Ray-Ban sunglasses that reveal no emotions; on his face is a cold, hard expression. I notice he has a black gun belt strapped tightly to his waist. He's probably annoyed that he's wasted his time chasing down some dumb kid who stole a boat.

"There are a lot of worried people looking for you."

Down in my little sailboat there are two crew men who are attaching a tow line and securing the tiller.

"Your parents are worried sick about you," he says, still

showing no sympathy. "Whatever made you steal a boat and sail off like that?"

Thinking fast, I say, "Well, school was over for the summer, and I just wanted to get out on the water to explore. An adventure, you know? I didn't think the people who own the boat would miss it because they never use it." I'm looking down at the deck to avoid his eyes.

"We're taking you back to Trent Harbor," he says, "where we'll have to turn you over to the authorities."

My heart skips a beat. I'm about to protest, and tell them about what I saw the mayor and the police chief doing, when he continues, "But first, can you tell me anything about a man by the name of Peter McMillan?"

I peer blankly at him.

". . . also known as Skinny Pete," he says.

"Oh," I say. "Skinny Pete? Sure, what do you want to know?" I'm relieved that we aren't talking about me stealing sailboats.

"We've been getting reports all summer that someone has been poaching lobsters from traps up and down the coast. We suspect it's him but, honestly, we don't have the manpower to follow up on it, or to even begin looking for him with 3,500 miles of shore line. That's an impossible task we don't have time for."

He continues on, "We think he was the one who radioed in

175

your location but we can't prove it. So, if you know where he was last located, we might be able to take care of your little problem."

I run a hand through my hair thinking about this. It's perfect. If I tell them about Skinny Pete, maybe they'll just let me go and forget about everything. Besides, Skinny Pete certainly didn't do me any favors.

"I don't know exactly where he is now, but I can tell you the direction I sent him."

"Sent him?" The first officer raises an eyebrow.

"He'd been taking lobsters out of the traps around Hunter's Island. I was helping him, but I thought they were his traps. I didn't know they weren't his." As soon as I say it, I realize that part sounds funny because, as far as trouble goes, that's the least of my worries. ". . . so I was mad at him. One night, when he was passed out, I drove his boat away from the island and towed a dory with me. When I thought it was safe, I hopped in the dory, put his boat into gear, then rowed back to the island."

I don't tell him everything because I think it'll only make matters worse.

The first officer looks like he's trying hard not to laugh. Then he regains his stern face, and says, "You know you could have put him in a lot of danger doing that."

"I know."

"So which way did you send him?" he asks.

"I think it was southeast. I didn't look too closely at the compass, but I think it was reading about 110 degrees."

"That's perfect," he says. The first officer's face turns from stone cold to a warm smile. "We know the radio range from when he called in your location so, given that we know the direction you sent him, we should be able to find Peter McMillan without too much problem."

He immediately picks up the mike of the VHF radio and calls back to Salem Beach Coast Guard station, giving them the last known location of Skinny Pete.

"That's great work," he says, giving me a slap on the back. His mood's certainly improving. "It's not like this guy is a wanted criminal, in fact, I think he's sort of a dill weed. But he's giving the Coast Guard a black eye with a lot of locals who're pretty upset when they find their traps tampered with or empty."

There's a slight lurch as the Coast Guard boat begins to move with my sailboat in tow.

"How would you like to ride up in the pilothouse?" he says in a fatherly way. "Come on, you can sit near the helm and Officer Jones can explain what he does."

"Jonesy," he says to the man steering the boat, "show this young man how our boat operates."

"Yes, sir," he snaps back.

I climb into the empty seat near Officer Jones and peer out

the window as we steer toward Trent Harbor. This is pretty cool.

∞ ∞ ∞

Before I know it, we're motoring through the Trent Harbor entrance. Off a little to the west, past some small islands, I can see a few of the guys are out for a sail at the sailing club, and beyond that, I can see the location of my hideout. I wonder if it's still there, or if someone has actually found it. Maybe Sara has turned it into a club for girls; I hope not.

Steering in a big arc, Officer Jones guides the Coast Guard boat in alongside the floating dock at the city pier, then momentarily reverses the twin diesels, bringing us to a neat stop. Two men jump off and quickly secure the bow and stern. We're back.

Before I leave the seat at the helm, I see through the window that my mom and dad are waiting for me on the dock. They both look nervous and excited. I take a deep breath, and then climb out of the seat.

Standing on the aft deck, I casually wave hello to the two of them, like I was just out for an afternoon ride with a few friends. "Hi, Mom and Dad," I say, and jump down onto the floating dock.

They both capture me in a big hug and my mom begins to cry.

My dad says, "Look at you, son! I almost didn't recognize

you, you've grown so much." He's right; I'm almost as tall as he is. My build's not yet as big as his, but I know I'm now plenty strong.

"Excuse me, folks, I need to take Fisher in for questioning." The voice has authority, and when I look back, I'm shocked to see Police Chief O'Reilly pushing toward me. His face is etched with a grimace.

I'm about to scream out but, suddenly, his powerful hand grasps my arm, squeezing tightly as he pulls me away from both my parents. I can't even breathe one word.

"Don't worry folks, you can see him as soon as we're done," O'Reilly says, pulling me away.

My mom begins to protest, but my dad stops her. Before I know what's happening, I'm sitting in the back of a patrol car, heading away from the dock.

After all this time, the men who I was trying to hide from finally captured me. God only knows what they plan on doing with me next.

« CHAPTER 17 »

Two Cherries on Top

Fear grips me like a tight, cold hand around my throat. It's hard to breathe. I'm imprisoned in the back of the black and white Plymouth Gran Fury patrol car with the man who's probably going to kill me. Certainly the mayor and police chief already have a plan in place; just like they must've had for the poor guy who was stuffed into the trunk of the old Buick. I'm shaking uncontrollably and want to scream, want to bang on the windows, want to do anything but just sit here. But with terror suffocating me, I can do nothing.

I'm stuck. There's no escape from the car because there are no door or window handles on the inside. Across the back of the front seat is a stainless steel cage, like the kind they use for kennels, to keep the bad guys from crawling to the front. This black and white has four doors—two for the good guys, and two for the bad guys-- and two cherries on top. Apparently, I am a bad guy. I'm a trapped animal.

After a minute or two of trembling in the back seat, while the officer talks to my mom and dad, I notice something reeks. I feel faint. At first, when I noticed the odor, I was pretty sure someone had peed on the floor. But now it's starting to stink more like someone has recently thrown up; the smell that makes you have to throw up too. The car's starting to get warm in the sun and there's no fresh air coming through the front window. I have to fight back that gagging sensation or I'm going to add to the stink.

Just at the point where I think everything in my stomach is going to come shooting out, Officer O'Reilly plops his fat butt into the driver's seat. He then starts the engine, and we drive off, sending fresh air my way. Just in the nick of time.

He doesn't say anything to me as he drives in silence; occasionally, I can see his eyes in the mirror glancing back at me. They're bloodshot, like he hasn't had much sleep. I stare at the back of his head, at the tight military haircut, and wonder how this could be the same man I remember coming to our school to talk. The man who showed up on career day was friendly and passed out Tootsie Rolls to all the kids. This Officer O'Reilly is unemotional, doesn't say a word, and gives off a sense that sends chills up my spine.

Sitting trapped in the back seat, my head leaning against the window, I'm not paying too much attention as we pass homes and stores. I've been away for most of the summer, but everything still looks the same. Trent Harbor never changes. Before I know it, we're whizzing past a large red brick building—the police station!

I begin to tremble again. "Where are we going?" I ask, banging on the cage that separates the front from the back. My hand hurts from banging and I try to shake off the pain.

In the mirror, Officer O'Reilly's cold eyes drill through me. "Don't worry about it."

But I *am* worrying about it; I'm worrying about it a lot! He's going to some deserted place where he can kill me, and no one will ever know. At least if we had gone to the police station with other people around, I'd have been safe.

Soon we're out of town and driving along a wooded, windy road that follows the shoreline to the northeast. It's been a long time since I've been on this road, but I think I remember where it goes. After ten minutes, we arrive. He slows the car down at a driveway, almost hidden with brush, where there's a plain black mailbox that says "Reed" on the side. Mayor Reed.

The house is offset a long way from the main road, surrounded by pine trees that make it invisible to anyone passing by. This is almost as bad as ending up in some deserted place. No one driving along the road will ever see us.

My face is pressed against the window, watching as we drive along the meandering private roadway and stop in front of the house. Abruptly, the car door swings open. Ouff! Dropping like a sandbag, I hit the driveway where fine crushed gravel embeds itself into my knees. Two solid hands grab my shoulders and lift me back to my feet. Just then, I notice crushed gravel is also stuck to my hands but, as I brush it off, it occurs to me my hands are free; Officer O'Reilly hasn't cuffed them.

Instinct tells me to run; run as fast as I can. To get away from him before he can catch me. Then my brain overrules; out here, the forest is so thick, I won't get far before they catch me. I stand stock-still and don't move.

"Come on, follow me," Officer O'Reilly says, as he gives me a shove forward. For some reason, I follow. Maybe when you're scared, your brain just locks up and no good ideas come to mind so you simply follow the guy who's going to kill you. This is not like the movies, where the sheriff mistakenly leaves his gun sitting on the table for the hero to grab.

We don't go to the front door but, instead, we walk around the side of the house to a wood-chipped path that leads down to a small dock. I can see down at the dock there's an old, wooden classic runabout powerboat, and on the opposite side, a little sailboat, almost the same size as the ones we use at the sailing club. Someone's down at the dock, but from where we are it's hard to tell. I'm guessing it must be Mayor Reed.

Is that their plan? To put me in a boat and take me offshore where they could shove my body overboard? I freeze. I can't move my feet. Officer O'Reilly stops in front of me, turns around, and orders me to keep moving. I do as I'm told.

When we're down at the dock, we stop in front of the powerboat. Highly varnished mahogany gleams in the sun. Any other day, I'd have been excited to have a look at the restored boat, but this is no ordinary day.

Inside the boat, sitting near the steering wheel with a white rag in his hand, polishing the wooden dashboard, is Mayor Reed. "Hello, Fisher," he says, when he looks up and sees us standing on his dock.

Sitting in his boat, he doesn't look very mayor-like; he's wearing some old, khaki pants that have a few blue paint stains on them, and his shirt is a simple green denim button-down shirt. The cap on his head was probably red at one time, but the sun has faded it so much that it's now more like pink. I don't think I've ever met the mayor before but, up close, he looks like someone's dad out of a TV show.

"I hear you like boats," he says, as he wipes his hands on the rag, then sets it off to the side.

I nod. I'm not sure I'm able to talk.

"Please, why don't you come aboard and sit down? We have some things to talk about."

Once again, I do as I'm told. I climb in, and sit in the middle row of seats while Officer O'Reilly climbs in behind me and sits on the far aft bench.

I need a plan, and I need it now. Over the past months I most certainly have grown bigger, and I'm much stronger than I was at the beginning of the summer. Could I take them? I could probably knock the mayor over into the water and run like hell, but the more I think about it, there's no getting away from Officer O'Reilly. He's big, and I know from being chased by him on that night long ago that he can be fast, too. That's a bad plan.

Brains, not brawn. Brains, not brawn.

Then, just like that, it hits me. Someone turned on a power switch to my brain and I remember I have a plan for this moment. I forgot I have a safety net.

"You can't kill me," I say, standing up in the boat. "Or everyone will find out about the guy you killed. Everyone will know! Everyone! Then you'll go to jail." I'm starting to tremble as I look defiantly at the mayor.

He looks truly astonished when I say that. "Kill you? You think we're going to kill you? I would *never* do that."

I stutter my words. "If something happens to me, I have a friend who'll mail a letter telling about everything you did, and it'll be sent to the newspaper. Everyone'll know. Everyone."

My mind's been a blank up until now with everything happening today, and I'd forgotten about the second letter I mailed to Sara. In it were instructions to forward it to the Portland Press Herald if anything were to happen to me. I'd even addressed it and put a stamp on it; if something happens to me, all she needs to do is drop it in a mailbox. I was quite proud of my plan at the time. But now? I'm not so sure . . .

The mayor takes his cap off and runs a hand through his

thick, black hair. "Well, I see." He looks out toward the open ocean for a moment and then turns back to me. "Again. I would *never* hurt you. And you thought we killed someone?," he asks, staring pointedly at me.

"How old are you?" he continues. "Fourteen, fifteen?"

"Thirteen," I answer. He nods.

Carefully, he thinks about what his next words will be. Then he looks me in the eyes, and speaks in a low tone. "Have you learned about the 18th Amendment yet in school?"

I stare at him blankly. I have *no* idea what he's talking about.

"Prohibition?" he says. I still don't know what he means, or where this is going.

He goes on to explain. "Back in the 1920s, selling alcohol was made illegal by the 18th Amendment. Even beer was included. The problem was that nobody wanted to stop drinking alcohol, so people started smuggling it in from other countries, like Canada, and Cuba. In the Smoky Mountains, people even built their own alcohol stills and were known as bootleggers."

"Oh, right." I said. "I remember watching an old TV show about them. I think it was called *The Untouchables*."

Mayor Reed continues. "Right. Well, here in Maine, people who did that were known as rum-runners. Some would sail up to the Canadian Maritimes, load up with whiskey, then sail it back to the States. All illegal, of course. Here in Maine, it was very difficult for the Coast Guard to keep tabs on all of the boats and where they were headed, so a lot of people did it. Some of the rum-runners on the Great Lakes would use speed boats, just like the one we're sitting in, to slip into Canada."

I understand all this, but I'm not sure why he's giving me a history lesson. "What's all this got to do with the body I saw you load into the trunk?" I ask.

"I'll get to that in a minute. There was a lot of money to be made as a rum-runner. Average working guys who owned boats, like fishermen, could become rich almost overnight. But keep in mind, it was illegal and very dangerous." The mayor pauses while he thinks about what he's going to say next, then rubs his temples.

"The body you saw us with was Elliot Woodridge; you probably know him as Grandpa Woodridge."

I never knew his first name was Elliot. Everyone, even older people, always called him Grandpa Woodridge. He lives in a big house on the other side of Trent Harbor. Maybe I should say *used* to live, because it sounds like he's not around anymore.

"Was he a rum-runner?" I ask.

"Yes, he was," answers Mayor Reed. "Grandpa Woodridge had an old coastal schooner that was pretty quick and had a shallow draft, so he could sail her into some pretty tight places. He and his small crew would sail her up to Canada, fill her holds with as much as she could carry, and sneak back in somewhere on the coast near here. In just two years he made a *lot* of money. But he was smart about it, and got out quickly before the Feds ever caught on."

Mayor Reed continues. "But he was one of the good ones. He did a lot of noble things for this town with all the money he made, and it helped everyone out a lot back then, especially because the Depression was just beginning. Even though Prohibition ended about 45 years ago, the federal government of today would probably not look kindly on his profession and there is a chance, albeit small, they could seize everything if they ever got wind of his past. We couldn't take that chance, even though that chance is small. It would be a shame if Joan Fennel lost the Sea Side because of something so long ago. We take care of our own here in Trent Harbor."

"Mrs. Fennel is family to Grandpa Woodridge?" I ask. "I was supposed to work for her as a dishwasher this summer."

"Yes, Joan is his daughter. And, a long time ago, he built the restaurant for her using his illegal rum-running money. She was pretty young then, probably only in her twenties."

"Would they really take her restaurant away?"

"They might. Who knows with the government?" says Mayor Reed. The whole time, Officer O'Reilly has been sitting quietly.

"When Grandpa Woodridge didn't show up for his Wednesday night card game, we knew something was wrong. Officer O'Reilly called me, and we both found him dead in his home. He simply died of old age. The thing is, we needed to give his place a 'clean sweep' to make sure there was nothing that connected him with his rum-running days, like old photos or paperwork. That kind of thing. It was necessary to look for anything that might catch the attention of someone outside Trent Harbor. Like, say, a newspaper reporter. But we needed some time to do a proper job of it. That's why we ran his body over to Jerry's Liquor Store to keep it cool for a few days while we quietly had a look around. I know it's probably not the most legal thing a mayor and police officer can do, but it needed to be done." He glances over at Officer O'Reilly and shakes his head.

This sounds really strange to me. "I still don't understand," I say. "Why did you chase me that night?"

"We were about to drive his body back out to his house so it could be . . . 'found.' That's when you came along. But you took off so fast we weren't able to explain the situation."

"So that's it?" I ask. "You chased me because you just wanted to explain what was going on? You didn't want to kill me?"

Mayor Reed shakes his head slowly. "No," he says.

"Here's the problem," the mayor says. "Nobody can know about this. I'll admit, it was all a bit outside the law, but it was for the good of the town. And do I need to remind you that you've stolen a very expensive sailboat? We'll look the other way if you look the other way. It's as simple as that." The mayor holds his hand out for me to shake. I certainly don't want any more trouble, and I think I understand what the mayor and Officer O'Reilly needed to do. This all feels strange to me, but I grab hold and give his hand a solid shake anyway.

"So what happens now?" I ask.

"We all just go back to what we were doing before any of this happened."

"Nothing will happen to me?" I ask again.

"Nope," Mayor Reed says, shaking his head. "I am truly sorry you thought we were going to kill you—it shouldn't have gotten that far out of hand. But I'm relieved you're safe now. Officer O'Reilly will give you a ride back to your folk's house. He'll tell them we just needed to ask you a few questions. Everything will be fine." I look over at Officer O'Reilly and he looks a little embarrassed.

The thought of keeping something like this a secret is incredible, especially since everyone's going to want to know why I stole a sailboat. It won't be easy, but it's far better than how I thought it was going to end. Suddenly, relief overtakes me: I'm going to live! Nothing's going to happen to me! I want to jump up and down, pumping my fist in the air, but I use all my might to contain my excitement. Emotion grabs hold of me. I turn away, hoping he won't see the tears that are welling up in my eyes.

I'll keep their secret. I just want to put it all behind me.

« CHAPTER 18 »

Paying the Price

Once again, I have *The Sticky Wicket's* wooden tiller in my hand. It's now like an old friend. We're moving through the water leaving a small wake behind, yet the boat's not heeled over, and there're no sails up to catch wind. My dad made arrangements with Gleason's Boat Yard to have one of the guys tow me back over to the home where I "borrowed" the sailboat that night.

And, if I know my dad, he also made arrangements for the owner to be there when we arrive so I'll have to explain why I thought I was allowed to take such a nice little sailboat. My dad doesn't know why I *really* took it. He hasn't asked. I made a promise that he or anyone else can never know. I'm just going to have to tell the owner I wanted to go on an adventure and hope it'll be enough of an explanation. But I know if it were my boat, I'd be outraged, and demand something be done.

My mind drifts back to the yesterday's events at the home of Mayor Reed. So old Grandpa Woodridge was a rum-runner? Now that I've had time to think about it, I think it sounds kinda cool; sailing a coastal schooner into Canada for illegal whiskey. I wonder why this is the first time I've ever heard about it? Why hasn't my dad ever spoken of it? He's lived in this town his whole life, after all. It seems funny now. I wonder if he knows but, like everyone else around here, wasn't supposed to talk about it. Maybe I'll ask him someday.

So I was just a dope who ran away when I saw trouble. I let out a heavy sigh as I steer the boat. But what if they really *had* killed someone? I still would've done the same thing. It was a dead body, after all. Maybe my imagination got the best of me, but I think I did the only thing I could have. Then I wonder about something that hadn't occurred to me before.

Because of this crazy misunderstanding, I changed a lot. I made myself get stronger so I could pull lobster traps, and I survived on my own. I don't know anyone my age who's done that. I even did a pretty good job of sailing and navigating *The Sticky Wicket*. I feel kind of proud of what I did. Maybe it was a good thing after all.

From my vantage point several yards behind the workboat's wake, I can see, around the corner, the rocky point where the summer home sits. "My" sailboat's real home. Although it's still far off, I can make out two older people, perhaps a husband and wife, standing on the pier as we slowly approach. It must be the owner. I take a deep breath and let it out slowly.

Just feet from the floating dock, the driver of the workboat casts off the tow line, leaving me to drift in slowly to the waiting people. I toss a dock line to each. The sailboat drifts to a stop alongside the floating dock. I give the workboat driver a wave and he's off, leaving me to answer the inevitable questions.

I try not to look at him, but the man appears to be in his seventies; yet he seems fit and trim. The well-kept white mustache on his face droops a little on the ends, and the navy blue sweater with tan pants give him the look of a true mariner.

After they secure the dock lines to cleats, the woman leans in and gives him a quick peck on the cheek. "Harold, I'll leave you two alone to talk." She turns quickly, going up the ramp, leaving the two of us with our eyes fixed on each other.

We don't say anything, at first. I turn and look out at the ocean, hoping to see something interesting that I can comment on. Nothing. I sigh heavily.

Folding his arms, the man slowly walks along the dock toward the bow, closely inspecting every inch of his sailboat. He still doesn't say anything and begins to work his way to the stern, this time rubbing his chin. Finally, after what must have been several minutes, he puts his hand out for me to shake. "Harold. Harold Plankinton," he says, in a deep-toned voice.

"Fisher Shoemaker," I say, more as a question, and I slowly reach for his hand to shake it. He gives my hand a solid squeeze; the kind that says I don't take crap from anyone, but I'm fair. I really don't know what to make of this situation.

He finally speaks. "It looks like you took fine care of my gal; the bronze is polished, and the woodwork is clean. I also see that all the lines are neatly coiled and in their place. That is the sign of good seamanship." He hasn't seen the other side of the hull that's facing away from the dock, where, the night I left, I scratched some of the paint. I've made a promise to myself to somehow get it repainted, but we don't need to talk about that yet.

"I'm told you sailed her all the way to Hunter's Island and back. That is very impressive, young man. I tell you what; I could not have done that." He gives me a smile that's genuine. He doesn't seem mad that I stole his boat; I'm not sure I understand what's going on.

He turns to me and says, in a more serious tone, "So it seems to me that we need to settle up on a little issue of payment for the time you used my boat. Any thoughts about that?"

All I have is the wad of money still left from hauling traps with Skinny Pete. With that, and working in the restaurant, I might be able to pay Harold Plankinton whatever it is he thinks is fair. I'm not prepared to pay for the use of his boat, but it's much better than the alternative of being sent to a reform school for boys.

"I've got some money, and I can work at nights in the Sea Side Grill. I had a busboy job lined up before I left. Maybe they'll still hire me back."

A deep laugh comes from him. "Look around, do you think

I need money? No, that's not really what I had in mind. You see, I've spent all my time in the city working hard and making good money. But I never had time to sail and certainly not on an adventure like you had. In fact, I don't even know how to sail, but I love sailboats; the way they look, the way it requires a man to know how to handle himself against the sea. I'm fascinated with it."

Climbing aboard the boat, he says, "I bought this sailboat because when I saw her, I fell in love with her. She's a beautiful boat." He strokes the varnished wood handrail as if he's scratching the ears of his favorite dog.

He continues, "I've always promised myself to learn to sail her. I just never had the time." Pausing, he looks me square in the eyes. "You would be the perfect man to teach me to sail her. You know her and what she can do; you've spent the summer on her. If you teach me for the rest of the summer to sail her, I'll consider that payment enough."

He adds, "Then, if it works out, I'll hire you on next summer to care for her and just have her ready to go if I feel like sailing. Do we have a deal?" Again, his hand is out for me to shake on it.

Certainly I do not need a second more to think about a deal like this! I grab his hand and give it a strong shake.

"Good. We can start tomorrow," he says, with a smile.

∞ ∞ ∞

Parked on the side of the road, just before the Plankinton's driveway, my dad is waiting for me in his car. I hop in the passenger's side. This is it, I think; I'm really going to get it now. But, instead, he says nothing. He starts the car and just drives back to town.

Before we get to Main Street, he says, "Do you want to get a burger?"

"Sure," I answer, a bit baffled. "Jake's Grill?" He nods.

So far, today's not turning out the way I expected it to. By now, I figured I would be halfway to some kind of severe punishment for stealing a boat and running away from home. But, here I am, about to go and get a burger with my dad.

Before we get out of the car to go into the restaurant, he says, "I want to hear all about your sailing adventure. All the details." My dad doesn't seem mad; in fact, he seems genuinely interested. This is not what I was expecting, but I'm pleased he actually wants to hear all about my summer. Just before we're about to open the door to the restaurant, he stops and turns toward me, putting his arms around me in a hug. Without a second thought, I do the same.

∞ ∞ ∞

The morning is sunny and bright with just a hint of fall in the air, which lets me know that school will start before I know it—like it or not. It'll only take me ten minutes to walk to the bookstore on Main Street where I told Sara I'd meet her. She phoned me last night to ask if I wanted to hang out today, and it sounded like a great idea to me.

I haven't seen her yet in the two days that I've been back, so I'm a little unsure of what to expect. In fact, I might be a little nervous. As I get close to the bookstore, I can see she's already there waiting for me. There're a few butterflies fluttering in my stomach. A deep breath doesn't seem to help.

"Hi, Sara," I say, now standing in front of her. Something about her has changed over the summer. For the most part she looks the same, well . . . maybe a little cuter, but she seems different in a good way. Maybe more mature? Maybe less annoying than when I first met her? I don't know what it is, but I like it.

She takes my hand in hers and we begin to walk slowly. "Want to go down to the waterfront?"

"Sure," I say. Suddenly, all the things I wanted to tell her over the summer evaporate like steam from a kettle. My mind goes blank. Why can't I think of anything cool to tell her? We walk in silence for three blocks.

Then I remember and reach into my pocket. "Here," I say. "It's your dad's jackknife that you gave me. It saved my life a few times."

"Really?" Sara sounds surprised. "It really saved your life? Then I'm glad I gave it to you."

I hand it to her. "You better keep it," she says, handing it back. "It may save your life again someday." We keep walking slowly toward the waterfront again, silent.

We pass two more blocks when she says, "I'm afraid I have some bad news."

"What is it?"

"It's about your hideout," she says. "It's gone. I went down there nearly every day to check on it for you, but there was one night when we had a bad storm and the tide must have been really high, and it just wiped it out. Gone. I'm so sorry."

I look ahead, thinking about my hideout. It's funny; hearing Sara tell me my hideout's gone doesn't really bother me. Over the summer, with all I've experienced, have I outgrown hideouts? It doesn't seem like a big deal anymore. It was certainly a cool hideout, but I don't really miss it. We keep walking.

As we approach the park across the street, a blue metallic color catches my eye. It's my bike, and riding it is Owen Scaggs! That little punk! I quickly realize he's a shrimp now compared to me.

Without thinking, I drop Sara's hand and sprint after him through the park. My speed startles even me. Luckily, he hasn't noticed me yet and isn't pedaling very fast as I overtake him. There's a curve in the bike path, so I dash across the grass, leap out from behind a tree, and grab him by the bike seat. The sudden stop sends him flying over the handle bars and rolling across the wet morning grass. Owen Scaggs has no idea what hit him.

Holding the bike and standing over him, in my best James Bond voice, I say, "Hello, Owen." There's a big green grass stain across his jeans where he skidded to a stop, along with a few leaves stuck to his greasy, black hair. His cigarettes are spilled out across the grass. The expression on his face tells me he has no idea who he's looking at.

"I see you're still using my bike."

He blinks twice. Then he starts to get up, but my foot holds him in place. He says, "Fisher Shoemaker?" In that same instant, he realizes I'm now bigger and tougher than he is. Owen Scaggs' face goes white.

"Hey, man," his voice quivers. "I haven't seen you all summer."

"Unlike you," I say, as he still sits pinned in the grass by my foot. "I'm not a thug who goes around stealing other kids' bikes." Reaching into my pocket, I pull out the roll of money I made from the lobsters, and peel off a twenty dollar bill. Slowly I wad it up into a tight ball and throw it at his head.

"I'm buying my bike back." With the bike in hand, I turn and walk away, almost daring him to attack me from behind. Instead, he just sits, with the wadded up twenty at his feet, too stunned at what has just happened.

I walk toward Sara, pleased with how things have turned out. She's smiling, too.

She asks, "Why did you give him twenty dollars for your own bike?"

"I don't know," I say. "I guess I just don't want to be like him. I know it's my bike, but somehow if I just took it, that would make me just like him. I don't want to be a scumbag."

Sara smiles, shaking her head. "You're a strange boy, Fisher Shoemaker." And she gives my hand a little squeeze.

∞ ∞ ∞

I'm sure I'll never forget this summer. It shouldn't have, but somehow everything worked out. Because of the crazy thing I saw that night, I now have a cool job teaching Mr. Plankinton, I made some cash on the run, I'm stronger and can survive in any situation and, somehow, I still have Sara. But there's one thing I don't understand. Why am I not in trouble with my parents?

The way I figure it, I should be grounded for the next ten years. I did a lot of things that weren't too smart. I stole a boat and ran away from home. There should be years of hard labor ahead of me, along with never trusting me again. But maybe there's something I don't understand about parents; maybe they're just thankful I'm back home and safe. Someday I'll probably get it.

There's one thing about this adventure that won't be easy, though. As strange as it is, I have a secret to keep. Maybe someday I'll spill the beans.

- *The End*

About the Author

MD Lee has sailed and worked with boats for almost forty years. In the late '80s he studied Naval Architect at the Landing Boat School in Maine. In the last fifteen years, MD Lee has also been writing articles for various sailing magazines. *The Boat Thief* is his first published book. There will be more Fisher Shoemaker adventures to follow.

If you liked *The Boat Thief* please leave a review. Also, you can visit Fisher's webpage at:

www.fishershoemakeradventures.wordpress.com/

On Twitter, please follow @mdlee62

34220464R00118

Made in the USA
Middletown, DE
12 August 2016